S0-BCL-363

WHITETOP PUBLIC LIBRARY
WHITETOP, VA. 24292

Also by Doug Swanson

Umbrella Man

Big Town

Dreamboat

96 Tears

DOUG SWANSON

HOUSE

OF CORRECTIONS

G. P. Putnam's Sons • New York

This book is a work of fiction. Names, characters, places, and incidents are either the product of the author's imagination or are used fictitiously, and any resemblance to actual persons living or dead, business establishments, events, or locales is entirely coincidental.

G. P. Putnam's Sons
Publishers Since 1838
a member of
Penguin Putnam Inc.
375 Hudson Street
New York, NY 10014

Copyright © 2000 by Doug Swanson
All rights reserved. This book, or parts thereof, may not be reproduced in any form without permission.
Published simultaneously in Canada

Library of Congress Cataloging-in-Publication Data

Swanson, Doug J., date.
House of corrections / by Doug Swanson.
p. cm.
ISBN 0-399-14615-6
1. Flippo, Jack (Fictitous character)—Fiction.   2. Private investigators—Fiction.   3. Galveston (Tex.)—Fiction.   I. Title.
PS3569 W2682 H68   2000   00-029669
813'.54—dc21

Printed in the United States of America

10 9 8 7 6 5 4 3 2 1

Book design by Bonni Leon-Berman

M SWA   1000147852
Swanson, Doug J.
House of corrections

Acknowledgments

I'm indebted to the book *Ray Miller's Galveston* (Houston: Gulf Publishing Co., second edition, 1993) for information on the island's history and culture.

Those with a keen knowledge of current Galveston may notice that I moved a few things around. I put them back when I was through.

Also, deep gratitude, as always, for the work of agent Janet Wilkens Manus and editor Jeremy Katz.

ONE OF THE MEN, a portly Cajun named Emil L'Hereaux, took a bullet in the forehead, a little left of center. The other, a skinny ex-con known as Mope, got his twice in the back as he tried to climb out a bathroom window.

The shootings took place about the time B. T. Mack ordered a slice of banana cream pie. B. T. was twenty-six years old and had been the part-time overnight deputy sheriff and jail guard in Luster, Texas, for almost three months. He had landed the job after a three-week career as a bouncer at a roadhouse outside Vidor, the next county over. B. T. lost the roadhouse gig when he punched the son of a local banker and knocked him out of his wheel-chair.

As a Luster deputy, B. T. had yet to see his first dead body, unless you counted his new girlfriend's grand-mother, who passed in a nursing home. He had gone to the funeral-parlor viewing, had gazed down at the old woman in the coffin. Somebody said she looked as if she were asleep.

"All plastered with makeup, with her hair combed nice and neat," B. T. said now. He was sitting on a stool at the Luster Truck Stop. "Sure didn't look like sleeping to me. They wanted that, they should've put the old lady in her pajamas."

"That's a awful thing to say," Cheri the waitress told him.

"Hey, *was* ain't *is*." B. T. ate his pie and watched Cheri's butt wiggle as she walked away. Two in the morning, nobody in the place but them and the cook. A sad song from the jukebox hung in the air along with the smell of old fryer grease.

B. T. cleared his throat. "Dead is an all-the-way kinda thing, know what I'm saying?"

Cheri wasn't listening anymore, so B. T. finished his pie and left. Out on the empty highway he pushed his patrol car to eighty-five, cruising toward the Luster Central Business District, with the East Texas pines flying by on each side. The little houses and ragged stores that clung to the edge of the asphalt were dark.

In a few minutes, he was at the shabby center of town. B. T. stopped at the flashing red traffic signal, corner of Main Street and Railroad Avenue, and gazed at some boarded-up windows. Talk about dead.

The thing to do now, he thought, might be roll back out to the county line and set up a predawn speed trap. Catch a quick nap that way, sunk low in the seat while the radar gun did all the work. He was about to go when he saw the other car.

It was, as B. T. put it later, hauling serious tail down Main, with its high beams blinding him. Now the car was half a block from him, still coming, not slowing a bit. With B. T. thinking he would be hit square-on, nothing he could do to stop it.

But at the corner, the car swung left toward Railroad Avenue. B. T. watched the red Camaro make a four-wheel, rubber-burning slide across the intersection. "Whoa, mama," he said, as the car skidded in front of him, hopped the low sidewalk, and wiped out a *Luster Advertiser* news rack. It stopped there.

B. T. grabbed his flashlight and ran to the Camaro. Finally, some excitement in this dog-ass place. He opened the driver's side door and shined the light inside. A woman's voice said, "It's a cop."

The driver was a decent looker, blonde. Blood dripped from her nose into her cupped hands. B. T. said, "You okay, ma'am?"

"I'm fine," she said, turning away.

B. T. shifted the beam to the passenger. She had short, dark hair, and she shrank from the light like an animal backed into a hole. He sniffed and got no smell of alcohol. Asking, "Anybody hurt bad?"

"I just told you we're fine," the blonde said.

"Soon as you stop bleeding," B. T. said, "I'm gonna need to see your license and your insurance."

He took one step back and counted up the citations he would have to write: speeding, failure to maintain vehicular control, no turn signal. B. T. was wondering whether to include improper lane change when the excited voice of the dispatcher came over the two-way radio that hung on his belt: Report of a disturbance with injuries, the dispatcher said, at the Carefree Motel.

Man, the burg was hopping all of a sudden. B. T. had no choice but to answer that call. He leaned into the Camaro, talking fast: "Your lucky night, ladies. Y'all are free to go."

The Carefree Motel was an old place out near Luster Building Supply. Ten units, cinder block, with a pot of sick petunias outside each door. B. T. had been there once before, his first week on the job, when a lodger on amphetamines was hauling chairs from his room and tossing them into the pool. Best fight B. T. had been in this year.

Now he blew into the Carefree parking lot with his red lights flashing. The night clerk, a wall-eyed vet of the Luster drunk tank, did a brittle-bones hustle out of the office. "Room five," he said. "I might of heard three shots."

B. T. blinked a couple of times, then gestured with his chin. "You been in there?"

The clerk shook his head. "Bullets start flying, I stay out."

"See anything from the office?"

"I was using the john when I heard it. Took me a minute or two to get clear."

B. T. narrowed his eyes. "Then how you know it was number five?"

The clerk sent the look right back. "Because that's the only one, junior, we got rented tonight."

B. T. took a big breath and let it out. "All right, then. Guess it's time to give a look."

"Think it'll be a mess?" the clerk said. "Velma's gonna be all over my ass if it's a mess."

B. T. paused by the pot of petunias outside the room. He drew his gun and held it by his ear, pointed up, the way he had been taught in cadet training. His flashlight was in the other hand. His shoes were so new they squeaked when he moved.

He knocked on the door. "Sheriff's deputy," he said, then said it again louder.

The clerk stayed about ten feet back. Saying, "She gives me any grief about damage, I'll quit her right now."

B. T. studied a quavery, tilted five that had been drawn on the fading turquoise paint with a Magic Marker. The door was pulled shut, but not all the way, with a sliver of dim light showing between the edge and the frame.

From behind him the clerk said, "Hey, I was looking for a job when I found this one."

B. T. pushed. The door swung open with a squeal of dry hinges. He stepped into a room that smelled of old mildew and fresh urine.

"Anything broken?" the clerk called.

A lamp was on, and the TV going. On the bed, faceup, was a man who probably went 250 pounds. He wore a Dallas Cowboys T-shirt that couldn't quite cover his belly, and white pants with a wet yellow stain around the crotch. Blood trickled from a dime-sized hole in his forehead.

B. T. felt the banana cream pie curdling. He stared at the fat man. This one definitely did not look to be sleeping.

He glanced to the rear, toward the bathroom, and saw a pair of legs dangling from the wall. One foot was missing its shoe. B. T. stepped closer, pointing the flashlight, and saw that the legs belonged to someone who had managed to get his head and shoulders through a window above the toilet.

Someone else must have decided he shouldn't leave. The back of the man's shirt was soaked with blood. B. T. lifted the tail of the shirt with the barrel of his gun and saw two bullet holes along the man's spine.

When B. T. came back outside, the clerk was waiting. Asking, "What's the report, junior?" B. T. pulled the two-way radio from his belt; dry mouth made it hard to talk when the dispatcher answered. Two fatalities, B. T. said into the radio. Gunshot wounds, lots of blood.

The clerk said, "Velma's gonna be pissed."

B. T. put the radio back in his belt, gave his head a hard clearing shake, and took a few deep breaths of night air. Then he watched as a black Ford Explorer bounded off the highway and into the motel lot.

It burned across the Carefree asphalt, going straight for the patrol car, not slowing down. B. T. put his hand on his gun. Telling himself, A night this crazy, no telling what else might bust loose.

The Explorer came to a stop three feet short of a wreck. The driver's door opened, and a short man climbed down. He was a stocky guy in his fifties, with a bald head and a full beard.

He moved quickly toward room five, waving a badge at B. T. and saying, "D.E.A., son. We'll take it from here."

It was all happening too fast for B. T. He stepped into the doorway and blocked entry. Asking, "Who are you?"

The man wore faded jeans and a blue nylon parka, with a snap-button western shirt stretched over a barrel chest. His forehead beaded sweat and his eyes jumped. He looked past B. T. into the room and said, "What's the situation in there?"

When B. T. didn't answer the clerk said, "Two of 'em shot to shit. Blood all over the damn place."

"Jesus Christ." The man looked like someone who had just been punched. "All right, step aside."

B. T. shook his head. "I'm gonna have to ask you to move away."

"Did you—" The man wiped his mouth with the back of his hand and rocked from foot to foot. "Did you or anybody else remove evidence from that room? Anything at all."

B. T. told him again to move away.

The man raised his badge to B. T.'s eye level. "See where it says Drug Enforcement Administration? You're right in the middle of a federal operation, boy. Soon as you crate your ass out of the way, I'll get on the phone with the Justice Department. F.B.I. crime techs'll be here the minute they can get a chopper in. And you"—he put his finger in B. T.'s chest—"you'll be lucky to keep a job cleaning toilets."

"Uh-oh," the clerk said. "Better let him in, junior."

The man said, "How much longer, boy, you gonna interfere with the United States government?"

B. T. thought of the way his high school football coach would tear into him when he blew a play. He remembered the coach asking him, How dumb, Mack, can one dumbass be?

He was aching to punch this guy, but B. T. was still a little gun-shy from his roadhouse firing. He swallowed hard and stepped aside, and the man blew past him into the room. The clerk whistled and said, "Must be something big."

"Open up that other room"—B. T. pointed to number six—"and let me use the phone."

He called the sheriff, woke him up. The sheriff said he was on the way as soon as he figured out where his wife put the car keys. B. T. told him about the federal agent. The sheriff said, "Do what now?" B. T. told him again.

"You instruct him to get his ass away from that crime scene," the sheriff said, talking loud. "I don't care who he is. You tell him that, and if he even looks at you cross-eyed, you place him under arrest. You copy that?"

B. T. copied it. Thinking, Goddamn, this'll be a pleasure. Maybe he'd be forced to slap the man around a little, even if it was a fed. He went back outside with his hand on his gun, ready for action.

But the Ford Explorer had disappeared. The night clerk stood where it had been.

"Looking for the bald dude?" he said. "Tell you what, he didn't waste no time. Took a quick trip through the room, pulled all the drawers out of the dresser, then lit out of here like his pants was on fire."

JACK FLIPPO WAS DRINKING at a long wooden bar, facing a big mirror on the opposite wall—always a poor idea, but especially bad tonight. Because in the silver glass behind the bar, above the terraced skyline of liquor bottles and below the hanging neon beer ads, was the reflection of Jack the birthday boy.

Thirty-nine years old tonight and what a smile, when he was smiling, which he wasn't now.

He drank his beer and gazed at himself. Big nose, small ambitions, shrinking chances. He needed a haircut, and he could use a new car. He was getting regular letters from the I.R.S. about $25,000 in back taxes. He had two ex-wives.

Jerry Lee Lewis, another old man with tax and love troubles, suddenly was singing "Middle Age Crazy" from the jukebox. Jack turned to see if someone was playing a joke, but no one in the weeknight crowd at the Tradewinds looked back.

He gazed over the mix of patrons and picked out the

people he knew: three bail bondsmen, a doughnut shop worker, a couple of full-time drunks, and a few bottom-feeding lawyers. It was the sort of clientele you might expect in a tavern on the unshiny side of Dallas, along a scabbed-over boulevard of massage parlors and industrial-supply wholesalers.

Jack heard an old man's voice say, "No one to keep you company tonight?"

Kelton, owner of the Tradewinds, had wandered over. Eighty years old, with a Chesterfield hanging from his lips: all smoke and wrinkles. Asking Jack, "Where's that young thing you used to come in here with? The one who wore all the hardware."

Jack took a swallow of beer and said, "Lola."

"How to describe her . . ." Kelton rubbed his chin with his palm. "Exotic would be the word."

Jack summoned the memory of her milk-white face, her green and purple hair, her tattoos, her head-to-toe rings and studs. "She moved out." He shrugged. "Gone, no forwarding."

"Yeah, I could see you looked a little down." Kelton thought it over for a while. "Well, the thing you gotta keep in mind, Jack, with these women, for every window that closes, another trapdoor opens. That's my way of looking at it."

Jack nodded. "Lola and I had a lifestyle conflict."

"Uh-huh. What's that mean, exactly? You don't mind my asking."

"She said if I really cared for her—"

"Here we go. Oh, they love that kinda shit, don't they?"

"If I really valued her as a person—"

"They'll drive you crazy with talk like that."

"—then I'd have myself pierced."

"Pierced." Kelton blinked a few times. "Don't get around, Jack, like I used to."

"Like they do with earrings. Only . . ."

"Oh, *that*." Kelton waved the air. "Hey, times have changed. It ain't just fairies anymore, Jack. Nowadays, lotta your manly sports stars got that crap stuck in their ears."

Jack shook his head. "Not talking about ears."

"Then what?"

"Talking below the belt. As Lola put it, every stud needs a stud."

Kelton smoked and stared. Then: "You're telling me, Jack, that she wanted you to get an earring for your dick?"

Jack peeled the label from his beer bottle and whistled with the jukebox. Kelton patted him on the forearm and said as he walked away, "For the rest of the night, my friend, you drink for free."

He downed a couple of on-the-house brews and left around midnight. A few miles down the road, Jack made the Edward Hopper scene at a tiny diner—greasy eggs from a waitress with a tubercular cough—then drove home.

A recipe for sadness and confusion: steady rain falling, heartbreak songs on the radio, alcohol and caffeine slugging it out in his bloodstream, the dark windows of an empty house as he pulled into the driveway. Jack wondered what he would say if he could unlock the door and walk in on himself, if he could stand aside and appraise his life with a cold eye. What would he think of his own sorry lot, other than he had a lot to be sorry for?

The phone, ringing as he came in, saved him from himself. Jack answered and heard the automaton female operator say, "Collect call from—"

A man's voice said, "It's me, you son of a bitch."

"Wesley? I'll accept."

"The one and only, back for more."

Jack thought of the last time he had talked with Wesley Joy, lawyer to the stars of scum. Over the years, Wesley had probably walked more felons than a prison break.

It had been a year since Jack sat in Wesley's law office, watching him try to crawl his way out of a hangover, listening as he explained why he was leaving Dallas. "It's just time to go," Wesley had said.

They had hugged when they said good-bye that afternoon. With his flowing silver hair, black eye patch, and grin to pick pockets with, Wesley in his fifties had been the best-looking reprobate Jack knew.

He also was a friend who had kicked some work Jack's way when he needed it. And at a low moment in Jack's life, Wesley had given him a place to stay. It led to other gifts.

Now Wesley said, "This old cowboy's been trying to reach you all goddamn night."

"The night's not over yet," Jack said, "so I don't see how that's possible."

"Got a job for you. You up for a job?"

"Maybe."

"I'm talking a big one. Maybe the biggest you ever had, Jackie."

"Right."

"You up for it?"

"Maybe."

"Bet your shorts you are. Listen to this setup: Man in a borrowed car—a *borrowed* car, Jack—gets lost, wanders into some piney woods tank town. Middle of the night, goes a little too fast. Cop pulls him over, finds a smidge of heroin in the car. Not enough in there to get a chicken high, Jack."

"And he claims it's not his," Jack said.

"Well, it's not."

"That's a new one."

"Cracker judge thinks he's got a big-time trafficker on the line, so he sets a half-million-dollar bond. You believe that? So here sits our victim of injustice, stuck in jail in Jesus Springs."

"Where?"

"Actually some dump called Luster."

"Who's in jail?" Jack said.

"You mean who did they screw, Jack? Who did they frame up? You mean what innocent man is behind bars right now, rotting his life away for something he didn't do?"

"Something like that."

"That poor unfortunate soul," Wesley Joy said, "would be me."

JACK PACKED HIS BAGS late the next morning and pointed his car, a used Chevy from a police auction, toward East Texas. With Wesley Joy in trouble, he really had no choice because Wesley had taken care of Jack plenty of times.

It started when they worked together as prosecutors at the Dallas County D.A.'s office, with Wesley the veteran and Jack the rookie. Wesley was a name around the courthouse, famous for doing whatever it took to make a case, notorious for his hatred and pursuit of all defendants. His motto was, Any fool can convict a *guilty* man.

Wesley showed Jack around, steering him clear of the office buttlicks and shiv-wielders, giving him the quick fill on which judges were hard-asses and which ones were lunatics. He taught Jack how to walk the minefields and how to dance with juries. And he passed on his personal secret to winning: Anybody ever tries to step on you, you steal his shoes. Then you chop off his feet. Then you make him walk home.

In the D.A.'s office, Jack and Wesley were *compadres* who watched each other's back. They stayed friends even after Wesley defected to the other side.

It happened after Wesley got rubber-drunk one night and drove his car into a hole that had been dug for a parking garage. He broke some bones and lost his right eye and spent weeks in Parkland.

"I laid in that hospital bed," Wesley told Jack later, "and I had a vision of God. The Almighty came down from heaven, Jackie, and he placed his divine hand upon my head and said, 'Wesley, working for the D.A. is no way to get rich.'"

So Wesley went for the big bucks as a criminal defense lawyer with a client roster of cash-hauling slime. Jack and Wesley were still close enough for Jack to tell him after a few drinks that he was saving the same shitbags he used to put in prison just so he could pick up five times the old paycheck.

Wesley looked hurt and said, "That's outrageous. You wound me, Jackie. I only do it for *ten* times the old paycheck."

Jack found out how good a friend he had in Wesley after he got hot for the wrong woman, a drug dealer's wife, and ran his lawyering career off a cliff. He left the law and tried to make it as a private investigator. The world didn't seem to be dying for a failed attorney turned low-end gumshoe. Wesley was one of the few who delivered for Jack when almost no one else would even return a call.

When Jack was broke and broken, Wesley had money to lend. If Jack needed work, Wesley found him some. If he wanted someone to talk with, Wesley was there to listen. This went on for years. A place to sleep? Wesley had a spare bedroom.

Jack, driving now to East Texas, thought about that spare bedroom. And about Wesley's wife, Angelique. And about Wesley's stare: Wesley had that one pale blue eye that would walk all over you and then burrow in. Jack had seen that stare take witnesses apart dozens of times. Once he had felt it on himself, like having someone open up a spy hole to your brain.

The last time Jack had seen Wesley was his farewell party. Wesley cashing out: He had made his stake; now he and Angelique were moving to the Gulf Coast. Going to buy a place on the water in Galveston, dabble in a little law down there, maybe get a small boat and enjoy life.

For the party, they had champagne and cake in the law firm's conference room while everyone made jokes about Wesley the pirate. Jack stood next to one of Wesley's associates and watched. Finally saying, "That Wesley, man, he's a great guy."

The associate looked back at Jack and said, "As long as he's on your side."

After five hours of driving, the last twenty miles a winding two-lane through swamps and scrubby pines,

Jack reached Luster, Texas. The town looked like something established by people who got lost in the woods.

Jack crossed a narrow muddy river, then cruised the main drag, a strip of smallville clutter. There were weedy used-car lots, a scattering of tired stores, and a couple of sagging catfish joints. Some log trucks rumbled and smoked, and the air carried the stink of a pulp mill.

He was looking for the jail. Most county seats had long ago grabbed some federal money and built new lockups on the outskirts, had put up some spacious, low-rise brick structures with electronic doors and video surveillance. Lots of room for everybody. What used to be the pokey was now the criminal justice center.

But Luster must have forgotten to apply for a government grant. Its jail still sat atop the old county courthouse, a two-story cracked-stucco box that held the center of the town square. Jack drove once around it—past the hardware store, the two-chair barbershop, and the Farm Bureau office—and parked in a spot under a dying live oak.

Inside, he climbed the echoing courthouse stairway to the second floor, where he talked to a sleepy, lonely sergeant in the sheriff's office. Jack flashed his bar association card—so what if he hadn't practiced law in a while?—and made vague noises about assisting in Mr. Joy's defense.

The sergeant sent him down the hall to the jail entrance, which was guarded by a young, fat, bored deputy. "Empty your pockets," the deputy said.

Jack dropped his coins and keys and Timex watch into a plastic dish. The deputy passed a metal-sensing wand around him and got no beeps. Asking, "You his lawyer?"

"Something like that."

"Got a business card?"

Jack fished a card from his pocket with one hand as he replaced his change with the other. He read the name tag above the deputy's pocket: B. T. Mack.

"I was the arresting officer," B. T. Mack said.

"Congratulations." Jack gave his face a glance; the deputy had a head the shape of a canned ham and eyes that seemed to be looking for someone to kick.

"This comes to trial," Mack said, "you'll probly be facing me on the stand."

Jack showed a make-peace smile. "Can't wait."

"I eat them smart-ass lawyers for lunch."

"Looks like that's not all you eat. You want to let me in?"

"I got a feeling we'll meet again," B. T. Mack said, "and one of us is gonna look like shit."

"One of us got a head start," Jack said. "Now, you gonna crack the lock, or do I have to go look for the sheriff?"

Mack put a key in the steel-barred door and opened it, then led Jack down a dank corridor, past half a dozen cells. He pointed to a metal folding chair set up just out-side the bars. Telling Jack while walking away, "Bang on the door when you're done, and maybe we'll let you out."

Jack turned to face the cell. "Goddamn, I knew you'd come," Wesley Joy said. They hugged through the bars.

There was a stoop to Wesley's shoulders now, and his hair had lost its salon-installed sweep. His nose was beakier than Jack recalled, his jowls droopier, his hands with more tremble to them. The pirate looked ready to trade his treasure maps in on a pension plan.

Wesley said, "Busts me up, friend, for you to see me this way."

He was wearing an orange jumpsuit and rubber san-dals, courtesy of the county. The cell had a cot, a stool, and a toilet. The floor was bare concrete, the plumbing stainless steel, and everything else painted an institutional green with a film of grime.

"Talk to me," Jack said.

Wesley shook his head and looked at the ceiling. "Here's my advice, Jack: Next time you borrow a car, make sure there ain't a tiny bag of heroin under the seat."

"I don't recall ever having that problem."

"And if there is, don't speed through East Texas rube towns. And if you do, don't get caught. Horse and crack-ers don't mix."

The inmate two cells down was having a coughing fit. Jack sat in the folding chair and leaned forward, shaking his head. "Last I heard you were living the good life in Galveston, you and your boat."

"We got us a thirty-two-foot sloop, Jack. Me and Angelique. Nothing to do all day but fuck and fish. Tell me that ain't the life."

Jack took a breath. "Sounds great."

"And then I get screwed, worst bad-luck day of my life, and wind up in here." Wesley glanced around the cell. "Remember what we used to call it? The S.O.D.D.I. defense."

"Some Other Dude Did It."

"Used to laugh our asses off at the losers who tried that one." Wesley rubbed the side of his face. "Well, some other dude *did* do it."

Jack leaned back and folded his arms. "What other dude did what?"

Wesley dropped to the stool and sighed. "I had business in Bossier City. But my car's limping, so Angelique borrows one from some friend, I don't know who. So far, so good. I thought I'd take a shortcut to Bossier, drove a little too fast. Next thing I know, the cop who stopped me is looking under the front seat and comes back out with a baggie. A smidge of heroin, ain't even mine, and all of a sudden these hicks think they got Pretty Boy Floyd on the hook."

Jack look around the jail: chipped paint, rusty bars, water stains, fluorescent light that didn't quite reach the corners. "Even in a dump like this, a half-million bond doesn't make sense."

"Look, Jack, I'm taking care of the lawyering myself. But I need you to do some of your poking around. That still your line of work?"

"It pays the bills most months."

"I want you to find my wife."

He had the pale blue eye burrowing into Jack. "I didn't know," Jack said, "that she was lost."

Wesley stood and gripped the bars. "She's on the goddamn boat. Somewhere in Galveston Bay, on my thirty-two-foot sloop, soaking up sun, not worried about a thing. Hey, for all she knows, I'm at Harrah's in Bossier, playing blackjack all day and catching the Mandrell Sisters at night."

"This boat doesn't have a radio? No phone?"

"I tried calling." Wesley rubbed his eyes. "She ain't answering."

"She dock it in a regular spot? Maybe you could phone there."

"She docks where she docks, Jack. Angelique likes to wander around."

Jack stood and leaned against the bars. "Why do you need her?"

"She can clear me, Jack." Wesley's voice was rising. "She can bring her friend in here—"

"To say what? That it was *her* heroin?"

"Look . . ." Wesley ran both hands through his hair, agitated. "I just want you to find her. Find the boat, find Angelique, then tell me where she is. That's all I'm asking."

Jack looked at the floor, shook his head, then came back to Wesley. "That's a big piece of water, Galveston Bay."

"Angelique doesn't do the open-sea bit, Jack. She hugs the shore, takes the boat to dock every couple of days. Hit the marinas around Galveston; you'll find her. Here." Wesley turned and picked through papers in a shoe box on a shelf next to his cot. Saying as he came back to Jack, "Picture of the boat."

Jack studied the photo. Angelique stood at the rail, smiling. She looked as good as he remembered.

"That's Lizette," Wesley said, pointing to a small woman next to Angelique. "She's our deckhand."

This is nuts, Jack thought. But he said, "All right," and he slipped the photo into his pocket.

Wesley said, "Somebody you might want to get in touch with." He passed Jack a scrap of paper with a phone number and name, Miranda Glass, *Galveston Tribune*. "She's left messages with the jailer. Wants to do a story on my case."

"How'd she find out about you?"

Wesley shrugged. "What difference does it make? All I'm saying is, maybe she can help you with the hunt." He put his eye on Jack again. "Look at me, Jack. One little bag of powder, not even mine, and I'm facing state time."

Jack saw a friend watching his life burn to the ground. "Sure," he said.

"Now I don't want you to tell Angelique what's happened, all right? I have to do that myself. I don't even want her to know I sent you. Just turn her up, tell me where, and let me handle the rest."

"Give it my best shot."

Wesley gripped his hands together and bent his knees, nearly dropping to the floor. Saying, "Do this for me, Jackie, and I'll never ask you for one more thing. But I got to have this one, brother. Got to. For old times' sake, huh?"

Jack left the jail and walked down one flight to the Luster District Attorney's Office. He figured he would have to make a nuisance of himself there before anyone would take the time to talk, saw himself cooling his jets all afternoon on a chair in the reception room. But Jack had it all wrong: He got a smile from the secretary and an invitation to see the boss right away.

The D.A., Billy Fletcher, was a thin middle-aged man who wore a vest and a red bow tie, who looked like the fussy president of the local Rotary Club: one of those guys always brushing lint from their sleeves. He greeted

Jack with a handshake, offered him a seat, asked if his guest would care for some coffee.

"So," Billy Fletcher said after introductions. "An investigator. All the way from Big D."

Jack nodded. "On behalf of my client, Wesley Joy—"

"Oh, yes." Billy Fletcher smiled. "The jailer let me know you were up there."

"Then you're familiar with the case."

"I'll say."

Jack cleared his throat. "Since the charge is a simple narcotics possession—"

"For right now," Billy Fletcher said. He flicked some dust from the crease of his slacks.

Jack cocked his head and leaned forward. "What's that mean?"

"It's what I like to call a fluid situation."

"And what's that mean?"

The D.A. laced his fingers on the desktop. "It's a moving target."

Jack knew he was about to take a kick in the ass, he just hadn't seen the boot yet. He said, "Half-million bond on a little bag of powder? Come on. For an attorney? An ex-prosecutor with a clean record?"

"Biggest bond in the history of the county." Billy Fletcher seemed proud.

"Hey, I'm all for setting records." Jack sat back in his chair and spread his arms. "But it wasn't even his car."

"I'll say."

"You'll say what?"

The D.A. shook his head and fingered a button on his vest. "Look, this was all laid out in the bond hearing this week. All on the record."

"I wasn't here."

"I'm surprised your client didn't tell you."

Jack didn't even know enough to mount a decent bluff. "He must have forgotten."

"I doubt that." Billy Fletcher rose, went to a metal cabinet, and pulled a file. "Seems to me he would have mentioned something this big."

The guy put on a show, giving Jack a slice of Billy Fletcher's courtroom drama. Thirty seconds passed while the D.A. looked through his file, whistling a little, finally plucking a single piece of paper from it. Saying, "Yes sir, believe he might have mentioned this."

Jack held out his hand. "I'd like to take a look at that."

Billy Fletcher said, "May I read it to you?"

"I can read."

"Please, allow me." The D.A. pulled half-moon glasses from his shirt pocket and slipped them on. Talking as if giving a speech: "Nine days ago a known narcotics dealer, one Emil L'Hereaux, was found shot to death at the Carefree Motel, right here in Luster."

"What's that got to do with—"

"As was his accomplice, Byron 'Mope' Edgar. Both gentlemen had lengthy criminal records. Assailants unknown."

Jack watched the D.A. preen. He said, "You want to get to the point here?"

"Now, the two unlucky men had arrived in Luster that afternoon in a 1997 Chevrolet, the tag number of which the motel manager recorded. Subsequent to the shooting, the car was discovered to be missing. I imagine you can guess the rest."

Jack could do more than guess; he could finish the story. But he didn't want to give the D.A. the pleasure of hearing him say it. He waited, with arms folded and hopes sinking, for the man to talk.

Billy Fletcher took his time dropping the paper back into his file. Then: "That car your client Mr. Joy was driving? When he was stopped for speeding in our fair town the next day? Seems it's the same one those drug dealers had driven to the motel. The one that disappeared right after they were shot."

The district attorney gave Jack a tight smile and said, "So the little bag of powder is the least of Mr. Joy's problems."

THE KIND OF DAY Miranda Glass had: up before dawn to hit the gym, only to find the gym closed. No explanation, just a chain on the door. She peered through the window to see a big, empty room, all the exercise equipment gone, vanished in the night like a caravan of gypsies. Along with the check she had written a few days earlier for a six-month membership.

Then on the road, driving Seawall Boulevard in her Jeep Cherokee, with the sun glittering the Gulf of Mexico. Squint a little and Galveston started to look like a real beach, almost, maybe if you closed one eye. There was a good song on the radio, hot coffee in her cup—the day might be saved after all. But then a bump—Jesus, the way the city maintained the streets, a fucking disgrace—and she had a fist-sized splotch of java on her khaki slacks.

To the office: a low cinder-block building on the backyard, bayside of the island, nobody's idea of beauty, but built to take a hurricane. About a third of the bulbs in the *Galveston Tribune* sign were burned out. The sign made Miranda think of afternoon lust fests in hot-sheet motels.

Not that she had been in any lately, though she had been invited just a couple of days before. Sort of.

It happened when she went on a nothing cop story, her punishment for mouthing off to the city editor, Ed Merritt. She had called Ed Merritt a putz, which he thought had something to do with golf until one of the old men on the copy desk set him straight. So Ed Merritt gave Miranda a week of night police.

That's how she found herself outside the Horseshoe Crab tavern, watching the cops arrest an old drunk who had tried to bust up everyone in the place. They had him handcuffed, shirtless, lying on his milky white, bulbous belly on the sidewalk near the front door. He looked up at Miranda, showed her a wide toothless smile and said, "Baby, once you been ate out with gums, you'll never go back."

Now she parked in the employee lot and walked into the newsroom: dingy blue carpet patched with duct tape, gray metal desks cluttered over, bare fluorescent lights that buzzed, stacks of old papers everywhere. A couple of editors had tiny offices behind plate glass. But everyone else, maybe twenty-five people in all when the place really got humming in the afternoon, sat together in the open, giving off low-wattage misery.

Only a few people were there now, sipping coffee, hunched in front of computer terminals. Miranda checked her mailbox—empty—and went to the hallway vending machines for orange juice and a blueberry yogurt. She was eating at her desk when she looked up to see Ed Merritt headed her way, always a bad sign.

He had his bland grin going, his way of announcing he was the most boring fucking guy in the world, and was happy as hell about it.

"Got a good one for you," he said when he arrived. "Friend at the fire department called this one in."

Miranda looked him over, saw a small-town guy who thought he could do GQ from Lands' End: slicked-back hair, black shirt, a burgundy tie patterned with flying ducks, gray slacks, and cordovan penny loafers. She said, "That outfit is ruining my breakfast."

"Why, thank you." Ed Merritt began to roll up his sleeves. "All right, here it is: Remember the big thunderstorm that passed through yesterday?"

"I remember it," Miranda said, "as if it were yesterday."

"Just before it blows in, two guys are out fishing on the bay, right?" He raised one foot and propped it on the rim of the trash can, showing Miranda a strip of skin and hair between cuff and sock. Miranda closed her eyes and pushed the yogurt away.

"Out in an open boat." Ed Merritt was still talking. "Big dark clouds coming, but our genius boys are not worried one damn bit, okay? Then one of them says, 'By the way, I'm getting married.'"

"I have another story I want to do," Miranda said.

"Second guy looks at the first one and says, 'Bullshit.' So the first one stands up in the boat, raises his right hand, and says, 'Hey, if I'm lying, God can strike me down.'"

Ed Merritt had the grin breaking over gray teeth. He said, "Guess what happened then."

Miranda said, "I got a tip about a Galveston lawyer in jail—"

"Are you going to guess or not?"

"—in East Texas. Heroin and murder."

"Last chance, Miranda. And one guess only. What happened to the guy who said, 'God can strike me down'?"

Miranda sighed and looked at Ed Merritt. "He got struck by lightning."

Ed Merritt's smile fell away. "How'd you know?"

"Shot in the dark. Listen, Ed—"

"Big boom," Ed Merritt said, "and the man's blown out of the boat. But get this, his buddy pulls him back in and the dude lives. They got him down at St. Mary's this morning in stable condition."

"Murder, heroin, local lawyer—can't go wrong when you have those in a story."

"I think it could be a great piece."

"You do?" Miranda couldn't believe it, Ed Merritt actually biting on one of her ideas.

"Hey, a guy says strike me down and that's exactly what happens? Great story."

Miranda and Ed Merritt stared at each other. "I was talking about the lawyer in jail," she said.

"I know you were." Ed Merritt nodded. "And I was talking about your assignment for today. Take a photographer."

Miranda did the story, not a very long one because the guy was bandaged like a mummy and loaded with painkillers, so he couldn't talk much. She got the interview late and busted deadline. By the time she was done, the only person answering the phone at the Luster jail was a sheriff's deputy who didn't want to talk.

So then home, thinking that the entire day had been a waste. It could have been worse: She almost had a wreck on Seawall when she changed lanes without looking. The other guy honked and Miranda gave him the finger.

The sun had been down a couple of hours when she finally made it to her house, one of those subdivision huts they put up by the hundreds in the eighties: brick veneer, three bedrooms, two baths, wall-to-wall carpet starting to show the traffic patterns already. Miranda flipped on lights as she walked through the near-empty living room and down the hallway.

The hallway was where Allen, her ex, had hung his Kiwanis plaques. Allen the accountant, whose favorite word was judicious. Who wanted Miranda to quit drinking beer and not to say "fuck" so much.

They had married in college and moved to Galveston afterward. It lasted almost four months. Allen fled to Houston, and Miranda kept the house.

Mainly she wanted it for the pool, which cost two hundred a month on a home improvement note from the wing-tipped loan sharks down at First National. Miranda walked toward the pool now, pulling her shirt away and dropping it on the floor, stepping from her slacks and leaving them on the rug. She left a trail of clothing to the back door and then outside. The last piece to go, her black panties, lay in a small silken heap at the pool's edge.

She walked down the steps and into the cool water, and then began to swim. Ten strokes and she reached the far wall. She pushed off, went ten strokes back the other way, then off the wall and back again.

The water flowed over and under her, between her legs and past her kick. It scrubbed the day off her. Motion kept her clean.

After half an hour, she climbed out. Miranda stood beside the pool, catching her breath and stroking water from her hair.

The wind gusted, scaling the water and perking her nipples. She glanced around, running her eyes across the six-foot wooden fence that enclosed her backyard. She could see the treetops of the vacant lot behind hers, and her neighbors' shingled roofs.

Miranda listened and heard nothing but branches thrashing in the wind: nothing but air on the move.

───────

The man in the tree belched quietly and got a souvenir taste of the chili he had for supper, Wolf Brand with beans. That's a dog, he said to himself as his gut rumbled, that's a dog that'll bark all night. He tried to remember if he had some Mylanta back in the car.

Ten in the evening, full moon, a little cool for July. But the woman was going for a dip: There she stood, beside the pool, pulling her undies off. Five seconds and she was naked as a fish.

The man wanted to say it out loud, Oh my baby baby. She was a little on the skinny side, but with a rack he wouldn't complain about. And she had a tasty-looking triangle of curlies down there in joy land. A sight worth the effort it took to get a fat man up a tree in the dark.

She stepped into the pool and began to swim, something the man had never learned to do. Back and forth, forever it seemed like, till his ass went numb on the tree limb. But better in a tree, he thought, than in the water. Nothing terrified him like the water.

Finally she was out, standing beside the pool in the light from the patio floodlamps, giving him all he wanted to see.

He put the camera to his eye; the big lens brought her up close, and he shot several frames.

The wind blew hard, and the man almost fell. The woman glanced in his direction for an instant but looked away. Didn't see a thing, he told himself.

She stretched and ran her hands over her hair, then walked toward her house. The man squeezed off a few more frames. Watching her move and whispering while he worked, "Honey, the things this big boy could do for you."

JACK SPENT THE NIGHT in Luster, taking a room at a motel favored by truckers who left their rigs idling all night in the parking lot. The walls felt thin enough to poke a finger through, and the couple next door fought like Tammy Wynette and George Jones after six diet pills and a pint of Seagram's.

The next morning Jack had some leathery pancakes at a nearby diner, then drove toward Galveston thinking about his last conversation with Wesley Joy: how after talking to the district attorney he'd gone back up to the jail, looked his old friend in the eye, and said, You didn't tell me anything about this shooting. Jack said, Two people dead, Wesley, and you're driving their car. Telling Wesley, You didn't mention one damn word about that.

Wesley smiled and said, I wanted you to find out for yourself.

With Jack looking back and asking, What's that supposed to mean?

Wesley gripped the bars, long thin fingers around the steel, and said, There's so much I don't know about this,

Jackie. I wouldn't presume to tell you what's out there, didn't want to limit you to knowing only what I know. He kept his stare on Jack and said, Somebody's trying to do something to me, somebody's after me, wants me put away.

Who? Jack said.

Wesley answered, That's all I can tell you.

His last words to Jack were, Just find Angelique. Angelique, Wesley said, can explain everything.

Anyone else, and Jack would have told him to forget it, would have turned around and made the trip back up to Dallas. Too much mumbo jumbo about mysterious somebodies and foggy schemes.

But this was Wesley Joy and Angelique, so Jack was headed to the coast.

What Jack knew: Galveston is a low, long strip of sand that its explorers, lost and storm-tossed, fittingly called the Island of Snakes. Indians who had lived there enjoyed reputations as cannibals. Jean Laffite, the pirate and slave smuggler, ran the place for a few years in the 1800s. Later, Galveston cultivated a long friendship with assorted bootleggers, gamblers, and whores.

The big event for the island was the 1900 hurricane. It bulled ashore with 150 mile-per-hour winds, blew for fifteen hours, and killed 6,000 people. There were bodies in ditches and bodies in trees. Not even the dead were safe.

The surging water ripped into cemeteries, unearthed graves, and sent coffins tumbling down the streets that had turned to rivers, until they splintered and spilled their loads.

Jack learned some of that in tenth-grade Texas history, taught by an assistant football coach who wore red knit shirts and red Sansabelts. He thought about the coach now as he drove across the long, arched concrete bridge that connected Galveston to the mainland. Then he saw the bay below him and, Jesus, there were boats everywhere. Jack forgot about the coach and mulled the task at hand: Finding Angelique Joy would be impossible without some help.

He hadn't been to Galveston for years. His father used to take the family down from Dallas when Jack was a kid, springing for three or four days at a motel near the beach. That was big spending for a man who owned a welding shop.

Jack remembered sunburns, putt-putt golf, and the old man's tales of vice dens. "That's Sam Maceo's old dice club," his father had said as they motored past a joint glimpsed at the end of a long pier. Twelve-year-old Jack took it in with awe, though the name Sam Maceo meant nothing to him. Guys throwing bones at some shack on the water? That was excitement enough.

He had always thought of Galveston fondly—the old, falling-down parts, at least. There was something about lushness, leaning toward decay, with a view of the Gulf of

Mexico. He loved the place after a summer rain: salt air, overgrown gardens, peeling paint, and the wet smell of rot.

The motel where Jack's family used to stay was long gone now, so he had to settle for a mom-and-pop lodge near Stewart Beach. It had free parking, the slight smell of mildew, and a toilet sanitized for his protection.

First thing he did was call the reporter Wesley had told him about, Miranda Glass. She answered the phone like somebody into the sixth month of a bad mood.

"Pissed off," Jack said to her. "I like that in a woman." She hung up.

Jack gave it five minutes, then called back. When she picked up he said, "I got your name from Wesley Joy." It kept her on the line. A few minutes of chat, and they agreed to meet that night for a drink.

Supper in the Luster Jail was peanut butter and jelly sandwiches, the same as lunch, the same as breakfast. Wesley Joy ate three of them, forcing them down. He would need the energy later.

Around seven o'clock, the deputies hauled in an old man who was drunk. They ordered him to remove his prosthetic leg before they put him in his cell. The old man pulled it off, waved it around like a hinged club, and yelled, "Gonna kick every ass in the room."

By nine o'clock, there were only two uniformed men left in the sheriff's department: dispatcher Othal Jackson and guard B. T. Mack. Evening thunderstorms were pounding away outside; the jailhouse roof leaked above the corridor along the row of cells. Othal Jackson put a coffee can on the old linoleum and positioned it to catch the drips. Then he walked toward Wesley, carrying a Bible.

Othal Jackson was a buck-toothed, pale man who looked to be a corpse-in-training, with a scratchy voice like something from a cheap speaker. He preached to the prisoners every night.

The one-legged drunk was muttering to himself in his cell, and the other prisoner—a truck mechanic charged with raping his fourteen-year-old cousin—stuffed toilet paper in his ears whenever the God-talk started. That left only Wesley to listen.

"Think that thunder's loud now?" Othal Jackson said. "Just wait till the Lord comes. We'll have horses with the heads of lions, beasts with serpents for their tails. See that can on the floor, catching rainwater? It'll be buckets of blood then, when the Lord takes his retribution."

Wesley sat on his bunk, watched the man talk, and thought about timing.

"And the fire will come down from heaven," Othal Jackson said, "and eat the sinners up. Amen."

Jackson closed his Bible, went away. Soon it was Mack's turn to stroll over to the cells. Usually he bragged about women and called his dick the big old East Texas hot link.

Tonight he said, "Thanks for the good words from the good book, Othal." Then to Wesley: "You won't be hearing them babies that much longer."

Wesley stayed on his bunk and said nothing.

"Soon as they get you a trial, Joy, get you convicted, be time to transfer you out." Mack smiled. "For some state prison time, the best kind."

Mack stood a foot from the bars and dangled a set of car keys from this thumb. "Chances are I'll be driving you over myself. That's gonna be one of my jobs, soon as I go to full-time, taking all our graduates to Huntsville."

"Fine," Wesley said.

Mack kept talking: "They's a good barbecue place I like to eat at on the way back home. So while them big colored prisoners is deciding whose girlfriend you're gonna be? I'm having a three-meat plate with extra sauce. What you think of that?"

Ned's Fish House hid on a Galveston backstreet, the sort of dive tourists wandered into only by accident. Jack remembered it as a place his father used to take the family for some cheap eats.

The current version had a couple of fifty-cent pool tables and a small kitchen. The cool air smelled of smoke and old beer. On the wall: high school football schedules and ad posters of big-busted black women holding cans of malt liquor. The clientele looked like a mix of V.A.

hospital outpatients and prisoners on work-release. Merle Haggard was singing from the jukebox. Jack felt at home the moment he walked in.

He took a stool at the bar, a few minutes early for his meeting with the reporter. "One draft," he told the bartender. He paused, then said, "And what the hell, a dozen raw oysters."

An old man in a T-shirt the color of nicotine shucked the oysters with a knife, put the half shells on a tray of crushed ice, and set them on the bar. "If you believe all the experts in the newspaper," Jack said, "this is like having sex without a rubber."

The old man picked up his cigarette from an ashtray, took a drag, and said, "Assholes."

Jack nodded. "Somebody's always trying to take the pleasure out of life. Seem that way to you?"

"Assholes," the man said again.

Jack mixed his sauce in a paper cup, horseradish and ketchup, with six dashes of Tabasco. Another Hag song came up, and the first oyster went down, salty and slick. Two swallows of beer, another oyster, and he was starting to feel himself come alive.

Maybe it was the food; maybe the music. Maybe it was just the sensation of walking free after seeing a jail cell. Whatever the cause, Jack's senses were finally opening up again. With all his usual problems left behind in Dallas, he felt as if he were surfacing from months of long, dark illness.

It was enough to make him want to commit at least a couple of the seven deadly sins, starting with gluttony. By the time the woman showed up, forty-five minutes late, Jack had downed four beers and two dozen oysters.

She introduced herself, Miranda Glass, *Galveston Tribune*, giving Jack a firm handshake and raised eyebrow. Asking him, "You always this pale?"

"A little bit bloated," Jack said. "You mind if we take a stroll, see if I can burn some of this off?"

They walked outside and around the block, past sagging Victorians with rusted wrought-iron fences and ragged palm trees. Jack tried to give Miranda Glass the once-over without staring: early twenties, on the tall and thin side, with short, light-brown hair and lips to stir the imagination. She looked like the kind of girl you could take home to Mom if Mom had a taste for girls who puffed Winstons and swore.

"Fuckface I work for thinks this isn't a story," she said, then blew a jet of smoke. "Has the imagination of a fucking gnat. Maybe you can help me convince him."

"Sure. You got any Alka-Seltzer?"

"No, I don't." She dropped her cigarette to the sidewalk and lit another. "So what's your deal in this?"

"Wesley Joy's a friend. I said I'd help him." Jack rubbed his bulging belly. "Man, I feel like a tire that's about to blow. I ate way too much."

"A swim would do you good."

That was the last thing he had in mind right now. "I didn't bring a bathing suit."

"Use your underwear. My backyard's fenced, nobody'll see."

Jack turned to face Miranda. Women had invited him home before—a few, anyway—but it generally took more than thirty seconds for the removal of clothing to come up.

She must have read the look. "This is an invitation to swim," she said, "not to screw."

"Now I see. You're one of those shy ones."

"I made some calls to Dallas, checked you out," Miranda said. "Plus I told a friend at work I was meeting with you, left her your name, address, and Texas driver's license number. So, they find my body tomorrow, all bloody and violated? Your name's the first on the suspect list."

"Lot of good that'll do you then."

"Anyway, you don't look like a killer." She stopped beside a red Jeep Cherokee. "In fact, right now you look like a little boy with a tummy ache."

She took keys from her purse and unlocked the Jeep. Saying, "Come on, I'll give you a ride."

Miranda drove like a maniac while talking about Wesley Joy. A tipster phoned her a week ago, she said, and laid out the bones of the case.

"This tipster say Wesley was innocent?"

Miranda shook her head and lit another Winston. "Actually the tipster said Wesley did it. Why?" She raised an eyebrow. "You think he's innocent?"

"That's what he claims. Who phoned you?"

"Anonymous female, that's all I know. Said she'd call again soon, but so far no comeback."

Jack felt a little woozy. He closed his eyes for a while and answered a few of Miranda's questions about how he knew Wesley. Finally Miranda said, "Here we are," and stopped the car.

"You mind"—Jack opened his eyes briefly—"you mind if I just sit here for a while? Rest up a little?"

"For what?" She opened the car door. "The twenty-foot walk to the house? Come on."

He followed her in and watched as she flipped on lights. "Give me a minute," she said and vanished down the hall.

The living room was bare except for a couch and a TV. Still, it looked like a good place to spend some time, maybe a year or so. Just as he was about to lie down, she was back with him, wearing a white robe and asking Jack, "What are you doing? The pool's out back."

He followed with rubbery legs out the door. The pool glowed with a shimmery blue light. Jack stood beside it and felt as if he might pass out. He turned and moved himself toward a patch of grass. The next thing he knew he was kneeling in it.

There was the sound of splashing. Miranda's voice said, "You coming in?"

"Maybe later," Jack answered. His voice had dead wings.

Cold sweat clung to his forehead. His stomach felt heavy and tossed around at the same time. He had visions of a brick bouncing off a trampoline and of a boat on rough seas. Then the big wave rolled in: He crawled on the grass and heaved his dinner into a flower bed.

When it was over Jack lay on his back, gasping. Something was dripping water onto his face—the woman, standing above him. She appeared to be naked. For perhaps the first time in his life that meant nothing to him. "You okay?" she said.

Jack shivered, hugged himself, rolled over, and retched some more. He had always wondered how he would die, and now he believed he knew: Poisoned by bad oysters while a nude woman watched.

The bells of a church near the Luster town square tolled at the top of every hour. Wesley lay in his bunk and counted ten chimes. Any minute now, he told himself, and she'll be here.

He rose and stretched, then stood at the bars, listening. Water still dripped from the leaky roof into the coffee can, and the rapist snored. And there was the faint noise of a television: the dispatcher's. Bubbling sitcom laughter made its way from Othal Jackson's cubbyhole down a hallway, through the tiny barred window of a steel door, and into the cells. To Wesley it was the happy noise of people who were free to move and came to him like the scent of food to a starving man.

Wesley had passed every night since his arrest this way. Unable to sleep, tired of writing, sick of reading. So he listened. His ears could pick up the scurry of rats in the walls and the skitter of roach feet across the cell's sink. Sometimes he believed he could hear the moans and howls of the men locked in this cell before him, their pain seeping from the walls like smells from a used mattress.

Other times he could hear only his own voice, telling himself all the ways in which he had gone wrong. At night his despair was like the lightbulb on the ceiling, always on. There was nothing crueler in jail than insomnia.

Now he waited and worried. At least fifteen minutes had passed since the church bell rang. The woman had never been this late before. Wesley imagined breakdowns and misfires, and he felt his guts in a clench. He was near the point of giving up when he heard the jangle of small pieces of metal.

The steel door at the end of the corridor opened on crying hinges, then clanged against the wall. Plastic casters rolled on the linoleum floor. Finally she came into view:

blond hair with dark roots, 150 pounds on a five-foot-three frame. She wore a red T-shirt that said, "I'm With Stupid," and stretch pants that covered her like a hot-pink second skin. The smell of Lysol came with her. To Wesley, she was absolutely beautiful.

She was, as always, pushing her mop bucket. Wesley smiled as their eyes met. He said, "Here comes that LaDonna." She froze. Wesley said, almost a whisper, "I was worried that something bad had happened. Nothing bad happened, did it?"

LaDonna shook her head slowly but otherwise didn't move. Wesley said, "Did your sister make it, too?"

The woman nodded. Wesley looked into those big brown cow eyes of hers and thought, She's about to drop her mop and run. "It's all right," he said, his voice soft, his hand extended through the bars. "Come on over here now."

She took one small step toward him and stopped, ten feet from his cell. "Do you have it?" Wesley said. "Show it to me. Go ahead, show me."

Wesley thought of what LaDonna had told him about herself over the past week, her life story delivered while she mopped. She was twenty-nine, with three children by two husbands. The first husband was dead, the second in state prison for robbery. She lived in a rusting house trailer that she still owed payments on. Her favorite TV show was *Judge Judy*. She and her sister, Belinda, had been cleaning the courthouse five nights a week for six months.

For Wesley, it had all added up to one truth: Give the woman a chance to make a few thousand in cash for one evening's work, and she would think she won the lottery.

Still, she was scared, and Wesley understood that. So was he. Now he said, "It's all right, baby."

Her right hand was clenched. "Show it to me," Wesley said again. He stared at her first, at the short fingers. LaDonna was a nail-biter. Wesley concentrated on her fist, beaming hard, like the guy who claimed to bend spoons with his eyes. "Don't be scared, now," Wesley said.

Slowly the fist opened, a flower blooming.

Wesley breathed out with relief. Resting on the woman's palm was a key.

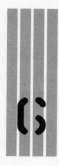

AT THE END OF his jailhouse sermonettes, Othal Jackson always told the inmates to give thanks in their prayers. Even the most woeful of men, he said, has blessings to consider. Wesley Joy agreed. Wesley was thankful that B. T. Mack couldn't keep his big old East Texas hot link in his uniform pants. And he was thankful that Othal Jackson enjoyed a nightly dump.

It had taken Wesley a week of talking to LaDonna, chatting her up while she mopped the floor outside his cell, to learn the whole routine. The way it went: Every night LaDonna and her sister cleaned the downstairs—the single courtroom, the clerks' offices, the tax division—then came up to the sheriff's department just after ten. That's when B. T. Mack took his new girlfriend, Belinda, into the sheriff's private office, to the sheriff's personal couch, and put the big hot link to her.

While that happened, LaDonna tidied up the deputies' rest room: wiping down the seat, scenting the air with Renuzit. Othal Jackson did not like a dirty toilet. When it was clean, Othal grabbed a fishing magazine and retired to the chamber for twenty minutes or so.

That left LaDonna in charge. Meaning that she was supposed to answer the phone if it rang. Also meaning that with Mackey humping and Jackson on the throne, there was no one to see if she slipped something to an inmate.

Now Wesley said, "Give it to me." He strained through the bars, almost reaching her, palm held upward. "Don't you want your money? One more baby step will get the job done."

He could hear her breathing. She glanced toward the open steel door that led from the cell area to the sheriff's offices. Losing her nerve, Wesley thought. He said, "Here we go, LaDonna."

Another hesitant step from her, a shaky extended hand. He almost had it, and then a snag: The phone rang in the radio room.

LaDonna turned toward the ringing, swallowed, and said, "Mr. Mack tole me I got to get ever one that rings."

"Let it go," he said. "Just this once."

"Mr. Mack said ever one."

Wesley knew that if she walked away now she wouldn't come back. She was close enough to touch. Wesley reached, grasped her wrist, and pulled her to him. LaDonna made a noise but didn't try to wrench away. He held her gently against the bars, looped his free arm around her, and put his face inches from hers.

She had crooked teeth, and her breath smelled like Doublemint gum on top of onions. "Give it to me," Wesley said.

LaDonna dropped the key; it sounded like a school-band triangle as it hit the floor inside the bars. Wesley released his grip, and LaDonna stepped backward. She fell over her mop bucket, and soapy water spread across the linoleum.

Wesley stooped and grabbed the prize. He was reaching out through the bars now. Pushing the key into the lock on his cell door. Turning it to the right.

But nothing happened. For an instant, Wesley felt as if he were watching someone close his coffin lid over him.

Then he twisted the key the other way. There was a lovely metallic click. Wesley pushed, and the door swung open.

LaDonna was on her back in the soapy water. Wesley left his cell and helped her up. He carried a three-foot length of homemade rope that he had fashioned by braiding strips of his bedsheet. He said, "You have something else for me?"

She slipped off her shoe—a sneaker with Velcro tabs in place of laces—and reached inside. "Hurt to walk on this thing," she said, handing Wesley a six-inch pocket-knife.

"You're beautiful." He took her by the hand. The ten steps to his cell were easy, like leading a trained pet.

"Sit there." Wesley pointed to his bunk. "Keep quiet." He left the cell and locked the door. "Don't worry," he said. "I won't tell them a thing."

Wesley walked past the other cells. His rubber shoes made no noise on the floor. The rapist was asleep, but the one-legged man had crawled to the bars. "Fetch my limb from the cabinet," he said, "and I'll run with you."

But Wesley kept walking, through the passageway where the steel door had been left open and into what the deputies called the operations area.

There were desks and file cabinets. Off to one side was Othal Jackson's table: a five-line phone, the dispatcher's radio, a black-and-white TV, and a coffeemaker.

The phone was still ringing; Wesley took care of that by pulling the wire from its jack.

He was turning to go when he heard a toilet flushing and the sound of water in the pipes. Next, a muffled cough. Wesley moved along the wall. A door opened, and Othal Jackson stepped out.

Wesley leapt before their eyes met, his forearm against Jackson's face. The two tumbled into the bathroom door and crashed through it. Wesley heard a splintering of wood, felt the two of them falling together, took a blow to the head sharp enough to make him see a burst of light.

Jackson lay on the floor, facedown, arms pinned under him. Wesley was on top. He put the blade of the knife against wrinkled skin at the back of Jackson's neck. All the fight went out of the man, as if Wesley had jerked the plug on a machine.

"And the last shall be first," Wesley said. He walked Jackson to the back and put him in the cell with La-Donna.

Wesley was breathing hard, could feel his heart pounding. At fifty-five years old, he was in no shape for fights. He moved past the cells again as the one-legged man said, "I'm begging you." Wesley kept going, down the cell corridor and into the operations room again.

The door to the sheriff's private office was still closed. He imagined Mack and Belinda inside. Wesley crept past.

He heard Jackson yelling from the cell: "Got a runner, Mack!"

There were two plate-glass doors in the front of the operations area, a red exit sign above them. Wesley had his hand on one of them, was just about to pull it open. "One more step," a voice from behind him said, "and I get to fire this baby."

Wesley stopped, then turned. Mack was standing outside the office door. He was naked, the big hot link hanging shiny under a huge belly. He pointed a pump-action shotgun.

"Only reason I don't put you down right now," Mack said, "is I'm on departmental probation for somebody else I done. Plus they give me ten fucking days of unpaid leave on that one, even though it only got him in the butt. Now drop that knife on the floor and get on over here."

He motioned with the gun toward a table. Wesley went where he was told. "Lean over," Mack said, "put your hands flat on the top."

Wesley placed his hands on the table. The dispatcher's radio was to his left, and Othal Jackson's coffeemaker, full of brew, was to his right. The coffee smelled old.

He felt the shotgun barrel at the back of his head. Mack said, "I heard that the last boy tried to run outta this place got a hole blowed in his kidney. So you the lucky one, Joy."

"Maybe you and I could make a financial arrangement," Wesley said.

"Oh, shit, Belinda, it's a rich boy. Wants to buy his way out." Mack pushed harder with the shotgun barrel, forcing Wesley's head down, his chin touching his chest. "I imagine you got some other kinda weapon in there somewhere," he said. "So undo that jumpsuit and drop it."

Wesley unbuttoned from chest to crotch. Mack grabbed the back of the collar and yanked. The jail jumpsuit was around Wesley's ankles. "The rest, too," Mack said. Wesley felt Mack's hand tugging his underpants down.

"Now lean all the way over on the table," Mack told him. Wesley had his face on the wood top. He could feel the heat from Jackson's coffeepot.

The shotgun barrel came off Wesley's skull and traced his backbone down to its end. He remembered for an instant the face of a client whose spine had been severed in a car crash.

"You got money on you?" Mack said.

"I can get it. Let me walk tonight; I'll have it at your house in the morning."

"Escape on credit?" Mack laughed. "That's a new one."

Wesley felt the cold steel leave his skin briefly and then come back hard, digging into his ass.

Mack said, "I feel the price going up right now."

Wesley clinched and squirmed. One shove from Mack and the gun would break the seal.

"Don't you try to move away now," Mack said. "Belinda, bring me them cuffs off the cabinet." The barrel started its push.

A woman's voice said, "What cabinet?"

"Over there," Mack said. "No, goddamnit, over *there*. Are you blind, bitch? Or just stupid?

For a second Wesley felt the pressure of the gun ease, could sense Mack's lifting and turning away. His one chance.

Wesley reached for the handle of the pot of hot coffee. He rolled and swung, shattering the glass across Mack's face.

Mack fell away, screaming, writhing on the floor with his hands over his face, screaming some more. He had dropped the shotgun; it lay there for the taking, and Wesley grabbed it.

Belinda, in her underwear, had backed herself against the wall. Wesley pulled his jumpsuit on, then gestured with the gun. Saying, "Go ahead and grab those cuffs now."

When Mack finally stopped yelping—his face slashed in a couple of places, his scalded skin showing splatter-shapes of bright red—Wesley said, "Now crawl. That way. You too, Belinda." Both went on all fours out of the operations area and down the cell corridor.

Wesley put Belinda in with Jackson and her sister, locked the door, and left them with a wink. Next he cuffed Mack, still naked, by one wrist to the bars.

( )n the way out, Wesley grabbed Mack's uniform from the floor and pulled it on—too big, but all right for night work.

He left by way of the plate-glass doors, each with SHERIFF'S DEPT in arcs of flaking black paint, and turned down a corridor toward a musty rear stairwell. It emptied into a dim first-floor hallway next to the circuit clerk's office. In seconds he had found the back door.

Wesley stepped into the humid, spongy dark and cut across the potholed parking lot behind the courthouse. Trying not to hurry in Mack's uniform, carrying the shot-gun. Looking, he hoped, like a deputy grabbing a break.

Bolivar Street ran off the square, deserted at this hour. Wesley took it, striding under the one mid-block street-light. At the far corner, parked head-in at Norma's Laun-drymat, was the car. As promised.

It was a beat-up white Toyota Corolla, probably ten years old, the kind of heap nobody would look at twice. On his knees, reaching into the front right wheel well, Wesley groped until he found an ignition key attached to a magnet.

He was about to unlock the driver's-side door but stopped cold. The car was white, but the door was red. So much for blending in. He felt his scheme start to turn black at the edges, like a leaf about to catch fire.

Wesley opened the door and slid behind the steering wheel. On the seat next to him were some neatly folded clothes and a paper bag. Inside the bag, he found a half-inch-thick stack of ten-dollar bills. At least that part had been done right.

Nothing to do now but hit the gas. Wesley took back-streets to the main highway. There, he had the road to himself with the car doing seventy, its little engine a high whir over the ripping sound of tires on wet pavement—like music. In a few minutes, the last lights of town fell away.

Pine woods were all around him now—unwalled, end-less space. He thought of the time in jail, of being let out-side for only one hour a day. The jailers called it the recreation period, when Wesley was allowed to stand on a tiny patch of cracked concrete at the side of the court-house, fenced in by chain-link and razor wire, a zoo animal on display.

Wesley's eye teared up as he drove. Soon he began to sob. He had not cried like this since he was a little boy. He was free.

MIRANDA'S CLOCK RADIO CAME on at six o'clock sharp, blasting the news of the morning in her ears before she opened her eyes. Terrorists had blown up a bus in Israel. A ferry sank in Sri Lanka, 200 dead. One California town was issuing each homeless person his own free shopping cart.

She rolled out of bed as a radio choir sang a jingle, happy as hell about their brand of headache relief. Speaking of sick people, she had a houseguest. Miranda walked down the hall to the spare bedroom. The man was sunk into the mattress, covers over his head.

"Yo, barfman," Miranda said. "Oyster boy. We need to measure you for a coffin yet?"

He answered with a groan. She stepped to the window and closed the curtains against the sunrise. Telling him, "Coffee in the kitchen if you want it."

She had finished toast and two cups by the time he staggered in. "You look like a zombie in a black-and-white movie," Miranda said.

The zombie seemed to be searching for a place to sit. Miranda took the garbage bag from a plastic tub and turned the tub upside down. "There you go, take a load off. Sorry, my ex-husband took most of the furniture."

The radio was on in here, too. After a car commercial, they had the Texas Gulf Coast forecast: high in the nineties with a good chance of afternoon thundershowers, some possibly severe.

"Which means," Miranda said, "that some sad-fuck reporter at the *Tribune* will have to write a weather story. The way my luck is running, it'll be me."

"Knock yourself out."

"The newspaper equivalent of cleaning toilets— weather stories. Unless the weather killed somebody." Miranda sipped her coffee, then said, "That happens, the story's worth doing. One dead, and you're probably on the front page. Two or more fatals, and you lead the paper."

"Fascinating." Jack rose unsteadily from the garbage can. "I'm going back to bed."

By seven o'clock Miranda was out of the house, wearing a silk blouse the color of café au lait, a pair of Guess jeans, and some silver earrings from a shop in Santa Fe. Shoes were ankle-high Gucci lace-ups that she had bought herself for her twenty-third birthday. They had pushed her Visa debt to saturation.

As she drove, Miranda kept her left hand on the steering wheel and her right on the radio buttons so she could bounce from station to station. At a light, she paused to hear two DJs badger a caller into giving thousands of listeners a description of her husband's private parts.

Another great moment from the wacky morning team. Miranda had interviewed them for a story once: a couple of paunchy radio lifers. One had a drunk's nose of broken veins. The other carried the look in his eyes of a man who would never do better than the dump he was working in now—and knew it.

The *Tribune* sign remained on the blink. Miranda was the first reporter in the newsroom again. She bought coffee, her fourth for the morning, and started toward her desk. A phone across the room was ringing. The stale smell of fried onions—the remains of dinner for someone on the late shift, stuffed into an overflowing garbage can—hung in the air.

She passed a gray metal table that was loaded with an unsteady stack of papers. On the top was a day-old copy of the *New York Times* with a photo that caught her eye. Miranda took it from the pile and studied a shot of rescue workers pulling victims from the rubble of a Central American earthquake. All she could see of one man was his head and an arm hanging limply from the wreckage.

Mass death and destruction in a distant place— Miranda burned to do stories like that.

She wanted her shot at great catastrophes in wretched lands. Miranda longed to describe the afternoon slant of light in the streets of Third World capitals. She wanted to write long, searching profiles of the leftist guerrillas, banana-republic dictators, and narco-traffickers she would meet. When the Ebola virus started mowing down Africans again, she planned to be there.

The closest she had come so far was a story on a measles outbreak at a Galveston elementary school.

Miranda started to put the paper back on the stack. But then she saw a byline, halfway down the page, above a story about New York City politics. She stared with disbelief at the name: Phyllis Patterson.

She suddenly felt like the guy buried in the rubble. Miranda had gone to college with Phyllis Patterson; they were the same age. And Miranda was ten times better. Shit, twenty. The only way Phyllis had been chosen managing editor of the school paper was to sleep with the editor. That's why they called her Syphyllis Patterson.

And now, working in New York? At the *Times*? While Miranda was stuck on some flyspeck Texas island, where you practically had to use ship-to-shore to contact civilization? Miranda had to sit down. Telling herself that maybe it was another Phyllis Patterson. That was a common enough name.

Her mind was spinning; she had to take deep breaths. There was only one way out. Miranda needed hot stories to grab the attention of big-city editors who would pluck her from Galveston—which, by the the way, smelled like dead fish.

She could begin with a story about a man wrongly accused of a crime: a lawyer, framed, stuck behind bars in East Texas. A piece like that could make a big difference. Maybe it wouldn't propel her directly to New York or Washington, but it might at least get her to Houston or Dallas.

That was a start. Wesley Joy, innocent man, could be her ticket north.

Ten o'clock on a steambath morning that promised a sauna afternoon. Angelique Joy sat in a deck chair on her boat and rubbed tanning oil on her thighs. She was drinking orange juice mixed with champagne, hoping for something to celebrate.

The thirty-two-foot sailboat was named *La Ventana*. It had been bought used for $144,000. Angelique had spotted it in a Galveston marina and fell in love right away. Telling her husband, Wesley, that all her life she had wanted to live on a boat. Persuading him to take out a bank loan. Wesley rounded up the down-payment cash, signed the papers, and *La Ventana* was theirs. Or hers.

Never mind that neither one of them knew the first thing about sailing. They could hire someone to teach them. An ad posted on the marina bulletin board brought Lizette their way.

Now the boat rocked gently on the slight waves of the marina. Crying gulls hung above a nearby fishing charter, waiting for someone to dump some chum. On the distant freeway bridge above the inlet, traffic was already heavy with people headed for the gray sand and green water of the beach.

Van Morrison sang on Angelique's CD player. She swallowed a Valium—doing everything she could to calm herself down, but not much was working. Angelique kept her eyes on the pay phone at the end of the dock.

Lizette was talking on the phone. Angelique knew this much about her: She was thirty-three, same as Angelique. Other things they had in common: the use of cocaine if it was around, and the failure to consistently wear underwear.

Unlike Angelique, Lizette could play the harmonica. She hated most men and loved all animals, while Angelique flipped that around. Lizette's big ambition in life was to set free the inmates of the fish prison at the Moody Gardens Aquarium. Angelique could give a shit.

Now Lizette hung up the phone and walked down the dock toward Angelique's boat. She was short with a grown-out buzz cut of dark hair, and had tanned, muscular legs. Her T-shirt said "Fur Is Murder." Lizette stepped onto the boat, scowling.

She leaned over Angelique's chair and said, "You won't believe this. He's out."

Angelique pulled her headphones off. "Out of what?"

"He broke out of jail."

"*What?*" The horizontal hold had broken loose in Angelique's mind. Finally she said, "That can't be true. Talked his way out, sure. But broke out?"

"I talked to the sheriff's department myself. They said he escaped last night."

Angelique's breath was coming in little packets. She stood and went down into the galley to look for Valium number two.

Lizette followed. "They're like, 'Who are you and why are you calling?' I said, 'Fuck you, goobers,' and slammed down the phone."

Angelique watched Lizette try to laugh. Then said, "All right, twenty-four hours, maybe less, he'll be sniffing around Galveston."

"Here he comes," Lizette said. "Nose to the ground."

Angelique thought about it. "The way I see it, he still needs us."

"In or out of jail, that doesn't change."

"It means we got to him, this escape. He's desperate."

"Unless he just takes off," Lizette said.

"You mean hide out the rest of his life? Change his name and lay low? No way Wesley Joy does that."

"Then he's got to deal with us."

"He'll be here sniffing around. Well, I can sniff, too." Angelique sipped her orange juice. "Know what I smell? I smell a big bag of money."

———

Jack felt as if he had been spending time on the underside of a slug. In the late morning, he managed to crawl from bed and walk to the kitchen on shaky old-man legs. His T-shirt smelled vile. He pulled it off, filled the sink with soapy water, and dropped the shirt in.

Queasiness still coated his insides. The muscles below his rib cage ached from hours of retching. His back was stiff from sleeping half the night on the bathroom tile, next to the toilet. Even his hair hurt.

In a nearly bare kitchen cabinet he found a can of chicken broth. Good thing it wasn't chicken noodle. He didn't have the strength to deal with noodles.

While the broth warmed in the microwave, he gazed out the back window. The blue pool sparkled in the sun. Jack was looking for his vigor, which he had left somewhere in the grass with the oysters. After half a minute, he had to sit down and rest.

The broth was done. Jack poured it in a coffee cup and took a sip, then another. Thinking that he might live after all.

The woman's house was short on furniture, but it did have that living room with the couch. Jack eased himself onto the cushions. As soon as he settled in, the phone rang. He made it back to the kitchen to answer, and all he got for his trouble was a hang-up.

From the couch again, Jack watched Jerry Springer on TV. Two large women, sisters in love with the same married man, tried to punch each other. Then the married man came out and they both tried to punch him.

Jack began to think of his two ex-wives and of all the pain he had caused them. That led to thoughts of other people he had hurt. He could feel their eyes on him now: Defendants of minimal intelligence and questionable guilt whom he had bullied to prison. A lonely woman he had laughed at and who had heard him laughing. A man who had pleaded for help and got Jack's back.

Over the years, he had ignored the lame, scorned the needy, and kicked the weak. Their faces floated through his mind now, a parade of those he had wronged. This took a while; it was a long list. Wesley Joy was in there, too.

THE ROOM AT THE Tweety Motel, on the interstate about ten miles north of Galveston, smelled of flea powder. Late-afternoon light oozed through the drapes. On the television a man was about to die of excitement because he won a riding lawn mower.

Wesley Joy lay on thin sheets on a swayback bed. Less than an hour after he fell asleep, he had awakened in a sweat, trying to climb out of a dream about himself in a hole with dirt pouring in. Wesley hated dreams.

Now he rose from the bed and stood over a rust-stained sink. He saw gray skin in fluorescent light, silver hair matted and dirty, and a bloodshot eye. The time in lockup had given his face more sag, as if gravity were stronger in a jail cell.

With a pair of scissors that he had bought at a convenience store near the Tweety, he began to cut his hair, shearing as close to the scalp as he could. Hair snowed around him, tickling his shoulders as it fell. When he was done, he soaked a towel with warm water and put it over his head, to soften the stubble. Then he lathered up and shaved his scalp.

A twenty-minute shower came next, as hot as he could stand, his first in weeks without a guard watching.

Wesley stepped from the bathroom, clean and bald, to find a fat man sitting on his bed and flipping TV channels with the remote.

"Congratulations, you made the news," Arthur Murry Murray said. "I heard it on the radio driving over. They're calling it a daring escape. You feel like grabbing something to eat?"

All right, fine, the car had a different-color door." Arthur attacked his plate of French toast in the Tweety Coffee Shop. They were sitting in a red booth in the rear of the place. "Hey, every now and then a man makes an honest mistake."

"A red-and-white paint job," Wesley Joy told him. "Not exactly an automobile that escapes attention."

"Ask you a question, Wesley. How'd you get the cell door open?"

Wesley sipped his coffee and waited.

Arthur said, "Had the cleaning lady slip you a key, would be my guess, after some friend passed her five grand. Same friend, be my bet, that left you a suit of clothes in the car. Clothes that don't scream jailbird, which represents an improvement over what you was wearing."

Wesley waved a hand. "You're right, Arthur. You did fine."

"No, you're pissed, Wesley, I can tell. You got steam rising off that hairless head."

Wesley set his cup down. "Someone might have seen me driving away. A car like that, they don't forget."

"Tell you what." Arthur raised his full moon of a face, still chewing. "For your next jail escape, I'll have a limo waiting. How's that?"

Wesley shook his head and looked out the plate-glass window toward the parking lot. He studied two eighteen-wheelers idling side by side and wondered what was in the trailers. He was thinking about all the places in the world you could hide things, about all the places where people could hide themselves.

"Limo and a police escort," Arthur said. "How about that? Maybe that'll—hey, I almost forgot. Brought you a present." He fished in his jacket pocket, then extended an open hand, palm up.

Wesley reached across the table and took a gold hoop earring from him. "My man."

"I knew you'd be missing yours after those Luster shits confiscated it," Arthur said. "Dude's gotta have his trade-mark, right?"

"Absolutely." Wesley slipped it into a hole in the lobe of his left ear. "How's that?"

"Wild Wesley the pirate is back." Arthur showed two rows of crooked teeth. "Except that with no hair you look like Mr. Clean."

Wesley picked up Arthur's sunglasses from the table and slipped them on. "How about now?"

"Now you look like blind Mr. Clean. Hey, speaking of cleaning. That cleaning lady did okay, huh?" He pointed with his fork to the remains of Wesley's steak. "You gonna eat that?"

"LaDonna," Wesley said. "I was afraid she wouldn't show."

"She'd better show, what she got paid. Five grand just to slip you a key while her sister spreads for the jailer? For that much, she oughta throw in a car wash. By the way, I got a look at the sister in daylight, Wesley. She ain't no grade-A piece."

"I was afraid they had flaked. They were late."

"Hey, Wesley, they made it, didn't they? And tell me this. How easy you think it was to go to this LaDonna— me, a guy she don't know from Fred Flintstone—and talk her into lifting the cell key and giving it to you? You think that was a snap?"

Wesley shook his head. "No, Arthur, I don't."

"It was your idea. I give you full credit, Wesley."

"And my money."

"That's right, your money, from your office, right where you said it would be. But making the sale, that was a bitch and a half. I mean, get this picture in your mind:

Arthur Murry Murray on some burgville shank's front porch, talking her into letting me in the house. And once I get in the house, I gotta figure out a way to offer her five grand to set you free while her sister does the poozle dance."

"However you did it"—Wesley lifted his coffee cup as if making a toast—"you did it."

"All them weeks I sold Amway," Arthur said, "finally paid off. . . . You gonna eat that?"

Wesley waved the food away as Arthur gathered bread from his plate. "Now," Wesley said, "all we've got to do is find the prize."

Arthur swallowed a mouthful and crammed more in. "You're speaking, I take it, of the lovely and elusive Mrs. Wesley Joy."

"She's around." Wesley raised his hand and closed his eye. "I can feel it. The bitch is in range."

This, Miranda thought, has to be the worst assignment yet: a feature on a retired Galveston used-car dealer who carved small statues of longhorns out of soap.

"One of his sculptures won first place at the Houston Livestock Showcase," Ed Merritt had said. "So you could write it as a local-boy-makes-good-in-the-city yarn."

Miranda had pleaded with Ed Merritt, which didn't work, then switched to hostility. Telling the dumb bastard she had a great story to do about an innocent man in jail.

Ed Merritt gave her the bland smile and said, "Go see the man with his statues. And take a photographer."

Now Miranda sat at her desk and steamed, waiting for the soap man to return her call. "He'll phone you in half a minute," the man's wife had said, "just as soon as he brushes his teeth."

Thirty seconds later, Miranda's phone rang. She took her time before answering with, "Glass."

"Hey, darling." A man's voice. "How you doing?"

"I've been better."

"I'll see what I can do to cheer you up. You wanted to talk to me?"

"So I've been told," she said.

"Where the hell should we start? You want to know how this old boy's feeling?"

Miranda watched the reporter at the next desk—fifty years old, looked like the guy who played Mr. Wilson on *Dennis the Menace* reruns. He was building a tower with a dozen coffee-stained Styrofoam cups.

"Do I want to know how you're feeling?" Miranda shrugged. "Sure, why not?"

"I'm real damn happy not to be in that place where I was."

"Uh-huh." Miranda put her head back and looked at the ceiling. Thinking, Great, a mystical soap sculptor. "Listen," she said, "we need to talk in person. And the editor wants me to bring a photographer."

A few seconds of silence. Then he said, "That won't fly, hon."

"Why's that?"

He cleared his throat. "As a fugitive, I got to be careful."

"A what?" She sat up straight, her feet flat on the floor. "You have to be careful as a *what?*"

There was a pause. "You don't know?" Then, "I figured a reporter might have access to the latest news."

Miranda whipped around to her computer keyboard and typed as fast as she could. Saying, "Give me a second," searching for the regional wire. A couple of key punches and it was on the screen before her: an A.P. story, dateline Luster, about a nighttime escape from the county jail.

She took two deep breaths. "It says here you injured a deputy."

"Believe you me," Wesley said, "the boy had it coming."

His voice was smooth and relaxed. She switched on the tape recorder attached to her phone and said, "Where are you?"

He didn't answer right away. "Maybe when we get to know each other better."

Two reporters near her desk were jawing about a movie, loud and laughing, making it hard for her to hear. Miranda flipped a hand at them. When that didn't work she barked, "Shut the fuck up." Then to the phone: "Why did you do it?"

"No choice."

"What are you going to do now? Where will you go?"

"I'm gonna show—" He paused. Miranda could hear traffic in the background. "I'm gonna prove," he said, "that Wesley Joy's an innocent man."

Miranda didn't know what to say. Wanting to tell the guy, You just pulled a jailbreak, for Christ's sake. "You're not serious."

"What's your idea, hon? Steal away and hide the rest of my life?"

"No, but—"

"My wife, Angelique, can provide my alibi. If I could only find her. Any chance she's been in touch with you?"

"Are you telling me you jumped the fence to find your wife?"

"Now you're cooking with gas. Here's my question: My friend Jackie link up with you yet?"

"We've met."

"Outstanding."

"I'd like to talk about it. Where can we meet?"

"I'll be in touch soon," he said.

"Wait, don't—"

He was gone.

———

Wesley sat in Arthur's black Chevy truck a mile down the highway from the Tweety Motel. "Don't mind telling you, I'm a little worried she might call the police."

"Who? The reporter?" Arthur Murry Murray rubbed his eyes. "She don't know squat about where you are."

"She could run the phone number back."

"And get what?" Arthur pointed out the window. "A pay phone at some no-place shithole Texaco? Besides, Wesley, she's on your side, remember that. You're the big story. She dimes you, what's she got then? The good citizenship award from the Galveston Chamber of Commerce?"

Wesley nodded. "You're probably right."

"You need her, and she needs you."

"I got to be real careful who I trust."

"Always true."

Wesley ran his hand over his smooth head. "She has an interesting voice." He thought about it while Arthur opened a briefcase. "Puts me in mind of a tough outer shell," Wesley said. "Not armor, really. More organic than that. What's the word I want?"

"Beats me," Arthur said.

"Carapace, that's it."

"Hey, that ain't all she's got." Arthur pushed a manila folder toward him. "Check these babies. Puts the hoot in hooters."

Inside the folder Wesley found half a dozen photographs.

"Okay, they're a little fuzzy," Arthur said. "I admit that. But for something I took at night—not to mention with no flash—they're not bad. Am I right?"

"Not bad," Wesley said.

Arthur laughed. "You shoulda seen me up in that tree, waiting for her to come out to her pool. Almost fell out and busted my ass. . . . The things I do for a naked woman."

Wesley studied the photos. "So this is the reporter."

"She puts the bun on the dog, know what I'm saying?"

"Maybe so."

"Guess what," Arthur said. "There's somebody can tell you for sure how much sweet meat she's got. Somebody who got the up-close-and-personal view."

"Yeah?"

"Been saving this one for you, Wesley, kinda like a dessert. Last night I'm staking out her place from the street; she comes home with a friend. And that friend would be"—he did a drumroll on the dashboard—"your buddy the asshole Jack Flippo."

Wesley smiled. "That's my Jackie, wasting no time."

"Guy must have spent the whole night at hump town." Arthur rolled down the window and spit. "I called her house this morning, and he's still there."

"Well, then." Wesley sat back and folded his arms. "It all seems to be falling in place."

BY LATE AFTERNOON JACK'S strength was on a slow fill, like a tub beneath a leaky faucet. He had enough vigor to dial his answering service in Dallas and find out that someone named Reece Pepper wanted to talk. Jack called the guy back and got nothing but a beep. He left a message and returned to the TV, watching gray-haired, post-liver-transplant rock stars reminisce about the glory days of drug habits and recording contracts.

Halfway through a sob story about Grace Slick—Jesus, she was as big now as the frycook at a West Texas Dairy Queen—Jack felt sleepy again; he took the phone off the hook and dozed. An hour later, he swam out of bad dreams about mollusks. There was the sound of a bell: not the phone ringing, and not his ears, but chimes from a plastic box on the wall.

Jack opened the front door and saw a short, round man, mid-forties, wearing tight jeans and a black Harley-Davidson T-shirt. Bald but with a dark beard, like someone whose head had been turned upside down. Saying to Jack, "You Flippo?"

"Why?"

He watched the guy look him over, then glanced down at himself: no shirt and rumpled, vomit-flecked pants with grass stains on the knees. Also, one sock missing.

"Guess it's true," the bald guy said. "Clothes *do* make the man."

Jack though he might say something about home delivery of dickwads. Instead, "Something I can help you with?"

A hand came out to be shaken. "Reece Pepper, Drug Enforcement Administration. Returning your call, in person. Cuts down on the cell phone bills."

"Drug Enforcement Administration?"

"Must be a mynah bird in here," Reece Pepper said.

Jack looked past the man and saw a Ford Explorer parked at the curb—black, with a brain-slicing sundown glare off the hood. He cleared his head enough to figure the scene: Reece Pepper got Miranda's number when Jack called and traced it to the house. "Just happened to be in the neighborhood?" Jack said.

The guy pulled his hand back. "Well, as it happens, I was in town, down at the Sportin' Life Tavern for afternoon vespers. Only about a fifteen-minute drive from here. . . . How about we chat?"

Jack gave it a couple of beats, then let him in. "Love what you've done with the place," Reece Pepper said. "The uncluttered look." He sat on the couch. Then, "Bet you know why I want to talk with you."

"Not really"

"Bet you could guess, you tried hard enough."

"Why don't you go ahead and tell me." Jack turned off the TV and sat on the floor. "Because I try never to assume anything."

"Good strategy," Reece Pepper said. "Puts me in mind of a famous saying: Never judge a man till you've walked a mile in his shoes. Because by then you're a mile away, and he ain't got no shoes."

Jack said, "You know, I'm not feeling too good this afternoon."

"Feeling pretty good myself, though them Sportin' Life cold ones is running right through me." Reece Pepper pointed toward the hallway. "Mind I go back there and drain the python?"

"Why not." Jack waved him back, then waited while the man did his business, watching through the front window as Miranda Glass's red Cherokee swung into the driveway.

Miranda came out of the Cherokee and crossed the front yard as if hornets were chasing her. Throwing open the front door with, "Did you hear? Joy broke out."

"Wait a minute." Jack got himself to his feet. "He did what?"

Reece Pepper came back into the room, wiping wet hands on his jeans and saying to Miranda, "Well, now, who's this?"

Miranda gave him an annoyed look. "I got a better question. Who the fuck're you?"

"I asked first."

"Broke out?" Jack said. "Wesley?"

Miranda said, "This dude a friend of yours, Jack?"

"We in your house, honey?" Reece Pepper sniffed. "Tell you something, that bathroom's a damn mess."

"Now I know who you are," Miranda said. "You're Martha Stewart's ugly brother."

"As in escaped?" Jack said.

"Yeah," Miranda said. "Where've you been hiding?"

"From the looks of him," Reece Pepper said, "I'd say under a rock."

Wesley Joy pulled his shoes off and sat on the Tweety Motel bed. "God, I'm exhausted."

"Breaking jail really takes it out of you, huh?" Arthur bit into a Hostess Ding Dong. "Never looks that hard in the movies."

Wesley lay back against a pillow and studied the rolls of fat on the back of Arthur's neck. Saying, "Something I never asked you. About the name, Arthur Murry Murray."

"Yeah, what about it?"

"Your parents meet in a dance studio or something?"

Arthur turned, chocolate crumbs on his lips. "I don't know what the fuck you're talking about."

"Never mind." Wesley settled into the pillow. "You know, the old days, on a big case, I could go for a week with no sleep. Sleep was for pussies."

"Know what I think they did?" Arthur polished off his snack in two bites. "Started making these Ding Dongs smaller."

"Your case, for example. No time for sleep in that one." Wesley smiled. "Remember Benny Dixon?"

"Don't remind me," Arthur said.

"Biggest little assistant D.A. in Dallas County."

"I drop turds bigger than Benny Dixon."

"You were gonna be his first capital conviction, Arthur. He told all the reporters he'd see you strapped to the gurney in Huntsville, watch while they put you down." Wesley laughed. "Mr. Big Shot."

"Benny Dixon"—Arthur picked his teeth with a fingernail—"was a beer fart."

"Then the jury comes back manslaughter, and poor Benny's about to cry on the spot. Next thing he knows, the D.A.'s chewing his ass about how he blew the case."

Arthur picked up the TV remote and flipped channels. "Hey, when I was in the Beto Unit—"

"Crown jewel of the Texas prison system."

"—when your friend, the asshole Jack Flippo, sent me down? That time? I bunked with a dude Benny Dixon convicted for agg assault. All he talked about was turning the tables when he got out. Said Benny had a kid."

Wesley raised himself on an elbow. "So?"

"So the guy later took a blade in the neck, bled to death in the prison laundry. Never made it back to rain on Benny or his family."

"He was gonna go after Benny's kid?" Wesley shook his head. "Man."

What Arthur thought but didn't say: That girl of Benny's was teenage pork chop. Sweet sixteen, poozle he'd pay to touch. Arthur, back in circulation, had stalked her for a few weeks. One night he made the Dixon back-yard via an unlocked gate and stayed outside her bedroom window for two hours, peering through a gap in the blinds. It was worth the wait: Arthur caught five seconds of the girl with nothing but panties on.

She worked Tuesday and Thursday nights at a Gap store, always parked her car in a spot that was just dark enough for Arthur's purpose. He was waiting for her there, ready to make a grab, when a security guard saw him. Took down the plate number before Arthur could leave in a hurry.

The next day the cops kicked Arthur's apartment door in, pushed him around a little, making noises about parole violation. For what? Arthur asked them. Parking in a parking lot? But that put an end to his plans for cute little Rachel Dixon.

Now Wesley said, "Wake me up in twenty minutes."

Arthur parted the Tweety curtains and took in the view of the parking lot. "Ask you a question, man."

Wesley kept his eyes closed. "Fire away."

"Why don't you just forget about finding your old lady?"

"Forget Angelique?" Wesley's eyes stammered open.

"Just cut to the nut, take your swag—wherever it might be stashed—and dive underground. New I.D., some plastic surgery maybe, you're good to go."

"Can't do that."

"What, you love her too much? Give me a break."

"Arthur"—Wesley sat up on the bed—"she is the one who can get me off the murder charge. You know that."

"Just offering a suggestion, that's all."

Wesley cleared his throat. Fucking lawyers, Arthur thought, always doing shit like that before making a big announcement.

"Suppose," Wesley said, "I'm caught. What then? Angelique is the one—well, her and that little lesbian Lizette—who can testify. So I have to have them if I'm gonna save myself."

"Fine." Arthur sighed and looked through the curtains again. "But this jerk-off Flippo better get moving, know what I'm saying? Hanging at the Tweety ain't my idea of a large time. I don't like staring at that swimming pool, and a man with my correctional history don't favor small rooms."

"Relax." Wesley lay back on the bed. "Jackie pays his debts."

Jack sat poolside with Reece and Miranda in the dusky swelter, each of them on a white plastic chair that still had the price sticker from Kmart. Plenty of talk, with nobody saying anything.

"So muggy out here," Jack announced, "you can almost swim in the air."

The sun had dropped low, time for mosquitoes. "Here we go," Reece said as he swatted, "the state birds of Texas. Or does the housefly have that honor?"

Miranda and Reece drank beer. Jack sipped ginger ale and wore a T-shirt that had been left behind by Miranda's ex. On the front: "Accountants Do It by the Numbers." He was feeling better now and had upgraded his own condition from pre-dead to feeble.

"You say you used to live near Houston?" Reece Pepper asked Miranda. "Ever go to the Laff Factory on Westheimer?"

"I had some creepy dates," she said, "but never that bad."

"I played there once last year, open mike night." Reece wiggled his eyebrows. "Hope to get a real gig soon."

"You're joking," Miranda said. "Comedy?"

"No, honey, striptease." Reece turned to Jack. "Lady wants to know if they do comedy at the Laff Factory."

Jack sipped his ginger ale and looked around the yard, first time he had seen it without poison bubbling inside him. The grass needed water and the bottom hem of the fence had gone ragged: termites.

"Of course I do comedy," Reece said to Miranda. "Under an assumed name, naturally. I mean, a federal narcotics agent can't exactly take the stage unless he has an alias. Guess what mine was?"

Jack said, "I'm gonna go with Shecky Preen."

"Actually, I started out as Malcolm Ex-Husband. Lately I'm thinking of giving the name Biggie Stud a try. Now, you ask: Reece, what kind of act do you have?"

"No, I didn't," Miranda said.

"I suppose I would describe myself"—Reece paused, building a moment—"as kind of a Texas-style Buddy Hackett of law enforcement."

Nobody spoke until Reece said, "So I challenge you, friends, to top that in terms of entertainment value."

"Well," Jack said, "I used to date a girl who painted a country-western version of the Last Supper. Conway Twitty was Jesus, and I believe Buck Owens was Judas Iscariot."

Reece nodded. "You could sell that to the crackers at every swap meet in East Texas."

"I'm going crazy." Miranda pressed her palms to the sides of her head. "Are we going to talk some business or not?" Then, to Reece, "I mean, why are you here?"

"My guess," Jack said, "is he's here because my name turned up on Wesley Joy's list of jail visitors. And yours, Miranda, was on the jail phone log."

"Good guess," Reece said.

"Or maybe"—Jack looked at Miranda—"the man dropped by just to discuss his Buddy Hackett homage."

"That would be special, wouldn't it?" Reece used a bare hand to wipe sweat from the top of his head.

"But police business has to take the driver's seat. . . . Chihuahua, it's warm. You mind I dip my toes in the pool?"

"Dip away," Miranda said.

"Speaking of the jail." Reece slipped his boots off and began to pull his white socks down. "I told them they needed to get old Wesley Joy into a more secure facility. My blind grandma could've busted out of the Luster house of corrections with her eyes closed."

Jack remembered his trip to the Luster jail: the tiny cell, the dim light, and the trapped-animal look in Wesley's face.

"Maybe he broke out," Miranda said, "because he's innocent."

"Innocent, that's a good one." Reece Pepper barked a fake chuckle as he rolled up the legs of his jeans. "I might like to try that one down at the Laff Factory, they give me a gig. All I've done so far is open mike night. I mention that earlier?"

Miranda picked up a net. She began skimming dead leaves from the surface of the pool and dumping them into the grass. Asking, "What's your case against him?"

Reece stood at the edge of the pool. "Reminds me of a story: two sailors pissing from a bridge into the river. One of them says, 'Damn water's cold.' Other one says, 'It's deep, too.'"

Miranda skimmed more leaves. "I just don't see that you have much."

"Emil L'Hereaux," Reece announced. "Byron 'Mope' Edgar. Two boys who used to be deep into the East Texas heroin trade. I'd been tailing them for three weeks, and all of a sudden they wind up shot dead. Then look who's got their car."

"You're telling us," Jack said, "that Wesley was running drugs?"

Reece shook his head. "I didn't say that."

Miranda put the net back in its rack. "Why would he kill two drug dealers?"

"Every one of us has his price." Reece rose from his seat and stood in ankle-deep water on the pool step. "I do. So does Wesley Joy."

Miranda, back with the chair and her cigarette, said, "What's that supposed to mean?"

Reece dipped water with a cupped hand and dribbled it over his head. "I baptize thee in the name of the father, the son, and the holy mackerel."

Miranda looked at Jack and rolled her eyes.

"Here's my theory, plain and simple," Reece said, "for all the plain simpletons in the crowd. Wesley killed them two boys and stole a little money from them. Which he then hid. Now he's laying low till he can grab the stash when nobody's looking."

Jack said, "He shoots them one night, runs away, and the next night he's back driving around Luster?"

"Maybe Luster's where he stashed the money." Reece went palms-up. "I've seen dumber stunts."

Jack flattened a mosquito on his arm, leaving a smear of blood. "Wesley's many things. Dumb's not one of them."

"I think he was set up," Miranda announced. "I think he's clean."

"Whoa, honey." Reece sighed. "You're way outta orbit on that one."

Jack watched Miranda try to keep the lid on. He could tell by her face she was dying to say, Who you calling *honey*, you fat fuck? But she had her hand out to the guy now, hoping for story material. She swallowed and said, "Why don't you set me straight, then?"

"Don't want the facts to get in the way of a good story, do you, darling?" Reece turned to Jack and winked, the same as saying, Watch while I give the bitch a few slaps.

"Just for the sake of argument . . ." Miranda pasted on a smile. "Is it possible that you and your narc buddies fucked something up, and now you're desperate to pin this on someone?"

"You through?" Reece said. Then, to Jack, "She through?"

"Probably not," Jack said.

"I can talk for myself," Miranda said.

Reece nodded. "I think we've established that."

Miranda dropped her cigarette butt into an almost empty beer bottle. It landed with a hiss. "All right, say he did kill them and steal some money. Why's he still hanging around?"

"What makes you think he's still around?" Reece said. "You talked to him since he busted out?"

Miranda looked away. "Maybe, maybe not."

"Listen here." Reece left the pool and walked toward them. His tiny feet left tiny wet prints on the concrete deck. "Talk like that, you might find yourself in front of a grand jury. I mean, the man is a fugitive, let's not forget."

Fugitive: Jack thought of Merle Haggard songs and *Cool Hand Luke,* of guys running through swamps, trailed by a pack of hounds. None of it seemed to fit Wesley Joy.

"And them grand jurors can be a tough room," Reece said. "Talk about someone that ain't in the mood to laugh. So I wouldn't write a newspaper story that said I knew where Wesley Joy was just yet, I was you."

"Pressured by the grand jury to expose a source." Miranda was nodding and looking into the distance. "That could go national."

Reece moved into her line of sight. "Which is the last thing you want right now, believe me." Reece caught her gaze and stepped closer. "You want every cop and every reporter in the state trying to get a piece of your action? Before you've had a chance to do it right?"

Miranda gave it a few seconds. "You making me an offer?"

Reece pointed. "Hold off a week before you write anything. Do that, and I give you the story."

"A week," Miranda said.

"Then I tell what I know."

"Everything?"

"And more."

Jack watched Miranda's face and considered the two ways of taking bait: Some spot the trap and beat it; some never see it until steel teeth are digging into a legbone.

"It's a deal," Miranda said.

Reece clapped his hands once and kept them clasped. "How about we seal it with another round? Wanna grab some more beers for us, honey? Some chips, too, if you got them. And bean dip."

She paused for a second or two—Jack could imagine her fighting the words, Get it yourself, fuckhead—then said, "Don't talk till I get back."

"Zip of the lips, right now." Reece ran fingers across his mouth.

She was in the house with a slam of the door.

"Whoo." Reece wiped his scalp again. "That girl's so far off base she ain't even in the ballpark. Which I suspect you knew."

Jack shook his head. "Not sure what I know at this point."

"Now that she's gone, let's talk." Reece winked again. "Man to man, here. Marine to Marine."

"I wasn't in the Marines."

"Me, neither. Just an expression."

"Then why not make it Elmer Fudd to Cary Grant? I'll be Grant."

"Whatever." Reece took a seat. "Listen, here's the true facts. When Mope and Emil walked into that Luster motel room, they was carrying a canvas bag. By the time I got there, that bag was gone. I believe Wesley took it."

"So now," Jack said, "I'm supposed to guess how much was in it."

"Save you the trouble." Reece finished his beer and swabbed his mouth with the back of his hand. "Mope and Emil was under the impression a big load of heroin was coming in, and they was gonna buy some."

Jack waited, mosquitoes buzzing his ears.

"Here's what I didn't want the reporter girl to hear." Reece leaned in close and dropped his voice. "I happen to know that inside that bag was—you ready for this?—a cool two hundred grand in cash American."

"Two hundred thousand."

"Is the mynah bird back?"

Jack stared into the man's small eyes. "And you think Wesley killed them for that?"

"I know people," Reece said, "who'd do it for less."

Jack glanced at Reece's hands; the guy chewed his nails to the nub. "So why are you telling me this?"

"Well—" Reece sniffed. "I could use the help, for one thing. Not like the D.E.A.'s only got one drug killing to chase, you know."

"Uh-huh."

"That look you've got right now? I've seen it before. I call it the what's-in-it-for-me stare. Also known as greed makes the world go 'round. Am I right?"

Jack saw Miranda through the kitchen window as she opened and shut cabinets. He got a memory flash of his first ex-wife, a woman who loved to dress up the kitchen with knickknacks. A wife who actually wore an apron and baked bread, for Christ's sake. He had wiped his feet on her.

"Here's your end," Reece said. "All that cash is subject to federal asset seizure and, your lucky day, the government happens to pay a finder's fee."

Jack waited.

"Meaning," Reece said, "you help me get that money back, ten percent is yours. I count my toes right, that's twenty thousand."

"Uh-huh," Jack said again.

"Say this, it'll buy you a pair of pants that don't have grass stains on the knees. With plenty left over for the finer things in life, like hundred-dollar hookers and Krispy Kreme doughnuts."

The sky was dark enough for the first glimmer of stars. People liked to talk, Jack thought, about the stars coming out when actually they had been there all the time. Stars shined all day, too.

Reece said, "So, you interested in coming along? We might even be able to increase your percentage, I talk to my supervisor."

"You want me to sell out my friend for a few thousand dollars."

"Did I say sell out? I don't think so. You can hang with him if you want, and after that you can go down with him. Hey, why wait? Maybe I should take you in right now, let you get lost in the system for a while, make sure you don't get in the way."

Jack watched the man and tried to remember all the times he had been shown the why-I-oughta bit by a cop. Something about this one was different, though.

"Good thing about it," Reece said, "is maybe you and your buddy can save money by sharing a defense lawyer. Speaking of lawyers, want to hear a good one? Know what happens when you give them Viagra?"

10

JACK SPENT THE NIGHT in his room at the Driftwood Motel. The next morning he made some calls, first
to his answering service to say he would be in Galveston
for a while. "Anybody wants me," he said, "have them
call my cell phone, or direct them to the Driftwood.
Unless it's the I.R.S."

Next he phoned every marina in the book, asking
about Angelique and her boat, leaving his name and
number should she turn up. Thinking as he did it, Might
as well throw a note in a bottle.

Then Jack called the D.E.A. office in Houston and
tried to ask some questions about Agent Reece Pepper.
Where was he based? Who was his supervisor? How long
had he been with the agency? Jack told them he was a
former assistant D.A., attempting to play the we're-on-
the-same-side game. He got through two receptionists to
the special-agent-in-charge, who told him the D.E.A. was
not in the mood to discuss, with perfect strangers, its per-
sonnel. If he wanted, Jack was told, he could file a written
inquiry.

All Jack wanted now was more sleep. Eleven o'clock in the morning, he lay back down and didn't get up until *The Tonight Show* was signing off. More than twelve straight hours he had been in the sack.

He showered, shaved, and put on some clean clothes. Gazing into the mirror and thinking that only a short time ago he looked like a complete loser who had lost the will to go on. But that was before he had slapped on the Aqua Velva. Now he looked like a complete loser who was still trying.

In a half-funk like that, there was nothing else to do but hit a late-night diner. Lucky for Jack, a Formica palace called Theo's sat right next door. Had to be good: The desk clerk, a guy with mysterious yellow stains on his shirt, recommended it.

Jack was about to leave his room when his phone rang. He answered and heard Wesley Joy say, "About goddamn time."

Jack sagged against the wall in surprise. "Jesus Christ, where are you?"

"In hiding. As befits a man of my fugitive status."

For a moment Jack couldn't get the words out of his mouth. There were too many of them—words like *escape* and *unbelievable* and *are you out of your fucking mind?* They bottlenecked in Jack's head like all Three Stooges trying to pass through a doorway at the same time.

Finally he managed, "You're insane."

"Not the first time I've heard that."

"Innocent people don't pull a jail escape."

"Old Wesley changed the rules."

"You could've at least waited until they convicted you." Jack sat on the bed. "Are you on the island?"

"Old Wesley broke the mold."

"You gonna answer my questions or do your act?"

"We gotta talk," Wesley said.

"We sure as hell do."

"We gotta map this baby out. Know what I'm saying? Our strategy, I'm talking about. Put us together a battle plan."

Jack saw himself in the mirror on the opposite wall. Say yes to Wesley now, he thought, do the aiding-and-abetting bit, and that's a felon in the looking glass.

Wesley said, "Are you with me, brother? Don't tell this one-eyed wronged man he has to pull it off all by himself. Do I have you by my side now?"

Jack breathed in and out twice. Then, "Riding shotgun with you, Wesley, all the way."

"Exactly what old Wesley wanted to hear, Jackie. Now, what's the news on Angelique?"

"Getting closer." Jack thought about adding, Maybe, more or less, relatively speaking, possibly. Instead, "Listen, Wesley, you and I have to sit down, hash this out. Figure out our next step."

"I believe I just said that." Wesley dropped his voice,

talking now like someone in fear of being overheard. "Just hang loose, Jackie, and I'll let you know the time and place."

"Let me know when?"

"Soon," Wesley said. Then he was gone.

▌hat last dump with the oysters wasn't lethal enough for you?" Miranda said. "You want to make another run at food poisoning?"

Jack had called her, suggested they meet. She had driven over, then waited in the Driftwood lobby while he strolled from his room. When spruced-up Jack walked in to find her, Miranda was pumping the clerk for dirt on crooked vice cops and bribe-taking city code inspectors.

"That guy knows plenty, but he's not talking," Miranda said as they crossed the parking lot to the diner. "Which is the usual problem with your bottom-of-the-food-chain workers. They know everything, but they're afraid to tell you."

"Maybe they're worried about their jobs," Jack said.

"I know the feeling," Miranda said. "*You* don't. But I do."

"Oh, yeah, silver spoon all the way, right here."

"Hey, Mr. Law School." Miranda thumped her breastbone. "You're looking at Sam Houston State University, working my way through the whole thing. All right, not the whole thing. End of my senior year, I married Allen."

"Fine," Jack said.

"But before Allen? Three years on the night shift at the Huntsville KFC, asking fat rubes if they wanted original or extra crispy."

"Sorry I mentioned it," he said, telling the truth.

"Six months to get the smell of chicken grease out of my hair. So don't fucking tell me about jobs."

Inside Theo's, Jack took a stool at the counter so he could watch the short-order cook. The guy knew what he was doing, a spatula master: cracking eggs onto the griddle four at a time, flipping sunny-side ups, cheap steaks done to a turn.

"This dude's good," Jack said.

"Spare me." Miranda, on the stool beside him, lit a Winston. "Listen, what do you make of this Reece Pepper?"

"Kept me in stitches. King of the dick jokes, far as I'm concerned."

"He's an asshole." Miranda blew some smoke toward the water-stained ceiling tiles. "Though you two seemed to be having a nice chat while I was in the kitchen. What was that all about?"

"Couple more jokes, that's all. Something about Viagra making lawyers taller. I didn't get it."

"I just don't know if I'm playing this right." Miranda reached for a pressed-metal ashtray. It was a sparkly blue that Jack remembered from high school majorettes' uniforms. "Agreeing to hold the story and all that."

"Do you have a story you can do right now?"

"Not really."

"Then you're playing it right."

"Thanks so much." Miranda ordered a cup of decaf. Then, to Jack, "Just what I needed. Advice from someone who knows absolutely nothing about journalism."

"All right, so I'm no Chet Huntley."

"There is no fucking way you are. Who's Chet Huntley?"

Jack shook his head. "Odds are Reece Pepper won't give you much of a story, anyway."

"You think I don't know that? He's a cop. I just want to be in line for whatever goodies he delivers."

"Wesley and Angelique. You get them together, that's your story."

"Hey, why else you think I'm sitting in this dive next to you? God, what is it, midnight? I gotta go home, get some sleep."

"Wesley and Angelique," Jack said again. Thinking that Miranda needed her story, Reece needed to make his case, while Jack needed—well, he needed a lot of things. "I just talked to Wesley."

She sat up straight. "All right, why didn't you say so earlier? What'd he tell you?"

"Only that he'll call me later. So it's standby for both of us."

Miranda sagged again and rubbed her eyes. "If I don't get some action quick, my career's about as dead as . . ."

She snapped her fingers twice. "Name somebody that's croaked."

"Huh?"

"My mind's fried, I can't think of anyone. Gimme the name of somebody that's stiffed out."

Jack shrugged. "I don't know . . . Chet Huntley."

"Really? That's a shame. Boy, the good go young. But that's how dead my career's gonna be, we don't get some action quick."

Jack, living large, got another pot of hot water for his tea and ordered two more pieces of toast. Thinking that there he was on his stool at fabulous Theo's, getting down and funky like a small-town librarian.

Miranda was a half hour gone, and the diner had lost all its customers but Jack and, in a booth near the cash register, a couple of lovers.

He gave the two a quick look. The man probably went 350 pounds and had the oily-haired, pockmarked, biker-with-a-drug-lab look down cold. The woman was boiler-plate meth-hag: peroxide blonde, skin and bones, eyes like broken-out windows. Every now and then she would set her coffee cup on the table and lick her boyfriend's ear.

The man must have had some kind of job going, and Theo's was his office. A phone sat on the counter next to his booth, close enough that he didn't have to leave his seat to answer. It rang every minute or two; the guy would reach for it, grunt, then write numbers on a napkin. Meanwhile his girlfriend drilled for wax.

On the jukebox: Dwight Yoakam singing "Rapid City, South Dakota." It was hard, it seemed to Jack, to keep your mind on a leash in a setting like that.

He turned and stared out the plate-glass window, toward the Gulf. There were small sets of lights on the horizon—shrimpers and channel markers. Jack was thinking about boats and open sea, harmless enough, and then his memory went over the wall and came back with the face of Angelique Joy.

The last time he had seen Angelique, she had a pink ribbon in her hair, a touch of little-girlishness that fit her the way a tiny cat's bell might fit an ocelot. They were having a drink in a hotel bar—the Adolphus, downtown Dallas—on a late afternoon. The two of them sat at a small table in the corner, with Angelique telling Jack about the big mistake she had made.

After fifteen minutes of nobody saying much, Angelique dropped her bomb: She had fallen for the wrong man. But it was all over now, she said, even though she loved him—probably *because* she loved him.

She had said that last part just as she got up to leave. Jack started to call to her as she walked away. But he didn't, and she kept walking. The next thing Jack knew, Angelique and Wesley had moved to Galveston.

Now someone was saying to him, "Look, you want it or not?" Jack turned to see the Theo's waitress, across the counter, staring at him as if he were a nasty spill she had to wipe up.

"What?" Jack said.

"Down there." She moved her head in the direction of the love couple. "Big Boy's got a message for you."

Jack glanced at the man, who was looking at him and waving a napkin. "For me?" Jack said. "I don't think so."

"Caller asked for the man at the counter," the waitress said, walking away. What little interest she'd had was draining fast.

"Uh-huh. Return to sender." Jack shook his head and turned back toward the window. Wondering if the lovers were trying to scam him, but not sure how or why. He watched their reflection in the plate glass.

Fifteen seconds later, the phone was ringing. The big man answered, then yelled, "Hey, asshole, I'm getting real tired of this."

Jack turned. Big Boy was holding a napkin again and staring his way. Saying, "It's for you. Like I got nothing better to do."

This one, whatever it was, wasn't going away. So Jack slid off the stool and walked toward the man. "The fuck am I, anyway?" Big Boy said. "The goddamn mailman? I got my own business to conduct."

"Something I can do for you?" Jack said when he reached the booth. He kept his eyes moving, watching for the sucker punch.

"Caller said it was an *important* message." Big Boy crumpled the napkin in his fist. "Cost you ten dollars to get it. Compensation for my time and trouble."

Jack was about to walk away until Big Boy said, "Dude said to tell you his initials was W.J."

Wesley again. He must have called the motel, and the desk clerk directed him to Theo's. "All right," Jack said and laid the cash on the table. "But for that kind of money, your spelling better be perfect."

Big Boy released the napkin. Jack picked it up, flattened it, and read, MEET 230 A M PELCAN I. SUB.

"Meaning what?" Jack asked.

The woman began to run her hand over Big Boy's crotch. Big Boy said, "Hey, you're asking me?"

"The person who left this message, he say anything else?"

"That answer," Big Boy said, "will cost you another ten."

The woman pulled at Big Boy's zipper. Jack didn't want to be around for whatever came next. He reached into his wallet and dropped a bill onto the table. Saying, "There you go. For the collection plate on Sunday."

"Your question, I think you said, was did the caller say anything else. Was that it?"

"Man, your memory's amazing."

Big Boy folded the ten and slipped it into his pocket. "The answer is no."

———

As a trained law enforcement professional, which he had been before getting fired two days ago, B. T. Mack knew the value of planning. So he had gone to one of those T-shirt shops on the Strand and bought a visitors' guide to Galveston. On page thirty-nine he found what he was looking for: the U.S.S. *Cavalla*, a World War II submarine.

That afternoon he drove across Pelican Island—a low stretch of sand between Galveston and the mainland, not much but scrub and marsh—to a remote city park bordered by a chain-link fence. There, the *Cavalla* had long ago been pulled from the water and half buried in the ground.

A couple of geezer tourists were gawking at the thing. B. T. took the steps that led from the grass up to the deck, and from the deck down into the boat. The outside of the sub was all rust and rot, but the inside was in pretty good shape. Even though it was cramped, musty, and hot, B.T. could walk from the crew's quarters to the torpedo room. From bow to stern, he told himself. Or stern to bow, he couldn't remember which was which. Hey, who the fuck was he, Cap'N Crunch?

The park closed at sundown. Which made the sub, it seemed to B. T., the perfect place to take care of business with this Jack Flippo.

Time for payback now, and how easy this had been. B. T. had called Flippo's office, getting the number from the business card the jerk had left him, and the lady said he was in Galveston. Which happened to be where the escapee was from. B. T. drove right over.

B. T. hated plenty of people—homies, homos, and ho's, to name just a few—but he especially hated mother-fuckers like this Flippo, and this Joy. Lawyers were scum, but the smart-ass ones were the worst of all.

A couple of times, when he was working as a security guard, he had been called as a witness in a case. It twisted B. T. up inside, the way the lawyers had smiled when they thought they had him trapped: baring their teeth at him. And the teeth were almost always straight and white, the mark of rich men from rich families. While B. T. had come up the hard way—pickup trucks that needed ring jobs, chickens scratching in the yard next to the satellite dish, a sister with a perpetual case of clap, a mother whose idea of supper for the kids was cold weenies straight from the pack.

He remembered the nights his daddy came home late and began to beat the kids one by one, starting with the biggest and working his way down. What was B. T. sup-posed to do—stop the old man in the middle of the whip-ping and say, Excuse me, Daddy, but do you have five thousand dollars to give me a smile like them rich boys?

B. T. would like to take some of these lawyers, get them alone, and pull those straight white teeth out one by one. Thinking now, Yeah, that might be the way to work it with the Flippo dude; instead of slapping him aroun with the butt end of a pistol, go dentist on the man.

He stood in the engine room of the submarine and imagined the scene: just the two of them down there, with B. T. yanking out Flippo's eyeteeth with a pair of pliers and telling him, Sorry, no painkillers available right now. Asking him while he cried and begged, You want to save the rest of your pearlies? Then tell old B. T. where he can find your friend, that one-eyed shit-ticket who brained me with the coffee and run off from the Luster jail.

So he had his plan. He drove back into Galveston, had dinner at Luby's—meat loaf, fried chicken, mashed potatoes, and two pieces of chocolate cream pie—then staked out Flippo's motel.

B. T., sitting in his car, parked fifty yards away, watched as Flippo walked to the coffee shop next door. He waited until the girl Flippo was with left. Then he walked to a pay phone, got the number he needed, and left the message.

Next he drove across Pelican Island again. Thinking, This'll be sweet. B. T. stashed his car behind some bushes and checked his watch—almost 2:00 A.M.—before using some wire cutters he'd bought to clip a hole in the park's chain-link fence. The place was deserted.

B. T. took the steps to the *Cavalla* deck, then descended into the blackness of the submarine. He had a penlight that kept him from falling on his face.

Next to the captain's quarters he found a table with cushioned seating on three sides. It was a tight fit, but he managed to squeeze himself in.

A little sign on the wall said the room was where the sub's commanding officers met to map their war strategy. Perfect, B. T. thought.

He put his pliers on the table and switched off his penlight. All he had to do now was wait for Flippo to take the bait. Except, shit, he'd left his gun in the car.

Miranda got her swim in, thirty minutes of back and forth, but skipped the nightly shower. Instead she rinsed the chlorine from her hair in the kitchen sink. Then she had a bowl of cornflakes. Thinking as she ate of all the places she would rather be. Dreaming of New York, but she'd settle for Houston. Jesus, at this point, she'd be happy with Waco.

Finally she was in bed, but was too tired for TV. Miranda set her alarm and switched her lamp off. She lay in the dark, with sleep coming on, trying to figure her next move. She wasn't sure whom to trust or which way to go. The only solution, Miranda believed, was to step on the gas and worry about direction later.

Full speed ahead, destination unknown—Miranda liked the feel of that. Maybe there was some adventure to be found in Galveston after all. It was a nice thought to send her to sleep, good as a good-night kiss.

But just as she was drifting off, Miranda heard the sound of breathing.

JACK HAD TO ASK AROUND and study a map, but he finally figured out what PELCAN I. SUB on the napkin meant. By 2:15 that morning he was driving over an old harbor drawbridge, then dropped onto Pelican Island. It was like walking through a furnished house and opening a door onto a dark, empty room.

A quarter-mile past the bridge, there were no street-lamps and no buildings. Just a bumpy two-lane cutting a straight line through the scrub, with nobody else on it. Jack did fifty as fat bugs swirled out of the cone of head-lights and splattered against the windshield.

Pelican Island seemed even flatter and lower than Galveston: land on borrowed time, waiting for the ocean to rise a few feet and take it back for good. A few glacier-melts near the poles, and the island would be a sandbar. From the looks of the place, nobody would miss it much.

In less than ten minutes, he was across the island, at water's edge, the end of the road. The park was there, like something someone put down a long time back and for-got to pick back up.

Jack pulled into an empty space—they were all empty—
and stepped from his car. A warm, moist breeze came off
the tidal flats. It smelled like a fish market on a hot night
after somebody forgot to pay the ice bill.

There were three lights: feeble pink on a pole at the far
end of the park, a sixty-watt job above a Coke machine,
and a flood on the ground, shining toward the sub. Jack
congratulated himself for having had the sense to stop on
the way and buy a flashlight.

The gate was locked, so he climbed the chain-link
fence—not that easy under the best of circumstances, but
doubly hard for a guy still running on fumes. He jumped
from the top of the fence and landed hard, his knees giving way like cheap hinges, Jack sprawling on the grass.
I'm turning into a joke, he thought, and not even a funny
one.

He got up, breathing hard, and a little echo of the old
nausea passed through him, just a few notes from the song
he had been dancing to. A man in his condition shouldn't
be climbing fences between midnight and dawn; he had
Wesley Joy to thank.

Your normal fugitive, it seemed to Jack, would go for a
parking garage if he wanted a secret meeting, the way it
was done in the movies. Or the underside of a pier,
which Galveston was lousy with. Not Wesley. Too easy,
too convenient. Too simple and lacking in drama. Why
choose the everyday rendezvous spot when you could

have a Captain-Nemo-up-on-blocks arrangement, sur-rounded by a fence?

Jack switched on his flashlight and played its beam over the sub. The *Cavalla*'s lower third was buried, as if it were just now surfacing from a voyage to the Inner Core. Rust had eaten away much of the outer hull, leaving steel ribs showing, like the bones of an old corpse.

He climbed the steps to the deck and got a nice view of the harbor channel. Half a mile away, the Bolivar Ferry was passing. A big wake, pouring off its stern, looked in the moonlight like a ragged rip in the water.

Jack went down the ladder and into the submarine; the only sound was his shoes on the steel. It was a cave in here: stale air and darkness that seemed to press in on him. All in all, Jack would rather be home right now, eating salty snacks and watching *Mannix* reruns. But he had no choice.

"Wesley?" Jack called, his voice banging off the hard angles. No answer came back.

Jack headed toward the rear, ducking and stepping through a hatch, banging his head as he went; these things were made for short guys. "You back there, Wesley?"

He heard something move behind him. Jack whipped around and pointed his light. On a steel shelf in the crew's quarters his beam picked up the shiny eyes of a rat. A rat that would have taken the blue ribbon at the tri-county large-rat show. A rat that seemed to be asking, The hell you doing in my house, chump?

Another moment of nausea rolled through him. He rapped his flashlight twice against a pipe, and the rat vanished into a hole in the wall. Jack turned and took a few more steps in the direction he had been heading.

That's when he saw the dead man.

The breathing came closer, someone drawing and blowing air through wet lips. Miranda sat up in her bed and tried to remember where she had left her gun.

It was a chrome-plated .22—the guy who sold it to her called it the divorcée special—and she usually kept it in the bottom drawer of the bedside table. But she had taken it from there the week before for a late-night assignment in a carjack part of town. She remembered slipping it into the glove box of her Cherokee. What she didn't remember now was taking it back out.

The intruder passed in front of the window: a large, lumpy silhouette crossing a faint rectangle of light. "Who are you?" she said. There was no answer but the breathing.

If she went for the phone, he would hear her. She could have tried to run but didn't think she would make it. The door had been shut; she knew that from the blackness of the room.

"What do you want?" Miranda said. Half expecting him to say, You know the answer to that. She reached down and opened the drawer of the bedside table, trying to be quick and quiet. Thinking, Please, Jesus, let me feel the shape of a gun.

All she got was a hairbrush, and she thought: I have no chance, he's got me.

Miranda ran her hand through the drawer in panic and desperation, finding curlers and combs as the intruder moved slowly closer. Her fingers wrapped around something made of metal. Not a gun; it was a can.

There was a rasping sound, and the room was no longer black. In front of the heavy breather's face, a tiny flame was flickering.

Miranda could see him now. He was holding a cigarette lighter.

The sudden sight of the body knocked Jack backward like a shove. A metal plate on the floor caught his heel, which sent him tumbling onto his ass. His head struck the steel bulkhead, and the flashlight fell from his hand. It hit the floor and went out. Jack heard it roll away from him.

He moved on hands and knees in the absolute dark, groping for the flashlight. His fingers brushed across something oblong and leathery; he touched it again, squeezed, and realized he was holding the dead man's shoe.

A few more minutes of crawling and feeling, and Jack closed his fingers around the flashlight cylinder. He gave it a couple of shakes, then rotated the lens cap a quarter turn, and the light flickered on.

Jack raised the weak beam of yellow light to the corpse. One wrist had been cuffed to an overhead pipe; the dead man hung from it like a carcass in a slaughter-house.

He was a large man with short dark hair and a scabbed, blotchy face. Maybe he looked familiar. Hard to tell now: His eyes were wildly bloodshot and bugged out, like a cartoon picture of drunken surprise, the way strangulation victims often are.

Now Jack lowered the light a bit and studied the rope. It was white clothesline cord and had been pulled so tight against the flesh of the man's neck that it looked like a tree cable over which bluish fleshy bark had begun to grow.

On the table next to him was a snub-nosed revolver and a pair of pliers.

The dead man had a paunch that sagged below the hem of his T-shirt, and muscular arms. Jack checked the man's back pocket and found a wallet. The driver's license gave him a name and a normal face, and it clicked: the Luster jail guard.

The dude was right after all, Jack thought. We did meet again, and one of us does look like shit.

He made his way to the front of the sub and climbed the ladder to the deck. There, he sucked in a few deep breaths of the salty air and tried to do a quick scope of the angles.

Two ways to work it: Jack had been the real target of the rope, but B. T. Mack wandered in and got it instead. That one didn't make much sense; if they wanted Jack they could have waited around for him to show, even after taking care of B. T.

More likely, Jack had been set up. That one tracked. The trail of phonied-up evidence was already in place—the phone call to Theo's, the note on the napkin, Jack asking around about how to get to the submarine. Wasn't hard to imagine someone phoning his name into homicide. And while Jack was out here on the island, someone could have cracked his room and stashed a length of the same rope they had used on B. T. The police would find it and match the fibers, case closed. Only question would be how many years he'd get.

So where were the cops? They should have been drawing down on him right about now. Yelling for him to freeze while they had ten or twelve guns pointed at his head. Maybe they were late. Maybe the phone tip got called in wrong, or the dispatcher screwed it up and sent them to some other abandoned submarine. That was the problem with these complicated frame-jobs, it seemed to Jack; one of the wheels was always falling off.

He climbed the fence to get out, hitting the ground without a tumble this time. Still no cops; Jack took a few seconds to look around. In the harbor channel the ferry was making its outbound trip. Otherwise, the place was empty and still.

His thought were flying too fast for him to catch them all, but he managed to nab one: If it was a setup, even a badly done frame, he needed to inoculate himself, had to have some exculpatory behavior to grease a no-bill. Best thing to do now, he thought, would be to notify the police. He could see himself, somewhere down the road, saying to a grand jury, Come on, you really think I would snuff the guy and then call it in from the scene?

Jack hustled to his car, ready to dial. A quick glance at the front seat and he realized he had left his phone in his room. So he looked around and spotted a booth about fifty yards away, beneath the single sickly pink streetlight. He sprinted for it, got there breathing hard, picked up the phone, and started to dial. The line was dead.

He pounded the handset so hard against the booth glass that it cracked into a starburst. Then thought, Wait a minute, maybe it's better this way. Since the police hadn't shown, he could see about doing a little more to dismantle the frame. Jack started his car and burned the road back to Galveston.

His hands shook as he drove; it had been a while since he had been surprised by a murder victim, and he was way out of practice. He made the harbor bridge doing sixty-five, flying over the bumps, scraping the oil pan a couple of times. Soon he was back in the neighborhood of the Driftwood Motel.

Jack parked two blocks away and approached the Driftwood on foot, staying in the shadows, looking for a stakeout, seeing no one.

He crept to his room, unlocked it, and swung the door wide before going in. The lights were on, just as he had left them. Nothing had been disturbed. He looked in the closet and under the mattress, but found no rope.

Now he drove back toward the harbor bridge, his setup theory on the wane. Still, there were witnesses—Big Boy being the star—who could link Jack to the submarine.

Jack stopped at a pay phone outside a liquor store near the bridge; this one worked. The dispatcher heard what he had to say, then told Jack to stay where he was and someone would pick him up. Three minutes later a cruiser was there.

It was another one of those kid cops. Were they recruiting them out of junior high now? Jack got into the car anyway. As they rolled across Pelican Island toward the park, Jack described what he had seen inside the *Cavalla*. The junior cop listened, then radioed his sergeant.

They waited in the patrol car, outside the submarine. Wasn't long before the sergeant rolled up, a paunchy guy in his late forties, bald, with a red walrus mustache. Jack wanted to ask him, A guy your age working the lobster shift? Who'd you piss off?

His name was Gowdy, and he asked Jack to repeat his story, which Jack did. Gowdy looked toward the sub. "Any chance he's still alive in there?"

"Not the slightest."

"Better take a quick look anyway."

Gowdy went to the gate and forced it open with three hard kicks, working like a guy used to busting in perps' doors.

Jack and junior stayed behind while Gowdy climbed into the sub. It gave Jack some time to work on his story, to come up with answers to the questions he knew he'd face: *Do you know the complainant?* He'd have to lie and say no. *What were you doing in there?* I got a note, he'd say, to meet a client. *What client?* The note didn't say exactly. *You expect us to believe that?* With Jack thinking, they didn't have to believe it as long as they couldn't blow a hole in it.

Gowdy came back in a few minutes, breathing a little hard from this trip up and down the ladder. Asking Jack, "You mind coming down in that thing for a minute, walking us through this?"

There's something screwy now, Jack thought, something Gowdy had found. It wasn't just setups that had trouble holding together. Cover-ups had the same problems. "Why?" Jack said.

"Just want to make sure I understand a few things," Gowdy said, "before we call the detectives out."

"Sure," Jack said. Thinking that at least he would know what the problem was; he'd be prepared for it when the detectives got him in a little room and tried to squeeze him.

He showed the two officers how he climbed down the ladder, and how he walked toward the stern of the sub.

Junior stayed in front of him, Gowdy to the rear. Both had flashlights.

Jack passed the shelf where he had seen the rat. "Shine your lights right there," he told them. They swung their beams in the direction he was pointing. What all three saw now: no handcuff, no rope. And no body.

"Oh, Christ." Jack felt as if his brain were spinning inside his skull. He turned to Gowdy. "Where's the dead man?"

"Same thing I was gonna ask you," the sergeant said.

After the police had gone from her house—it had taken a couple of hours for them to finish talking to her and to do a crime scene—Miranda drove to her office. She walked straight to her desk, logged on to her computer, and began to write.

By 9:00 A.M. she had filed her story, a first-person piece that ran at the top of page one in that afternoon's editions. The headline: REPORTER RECOUNTS NIGHT OF TERROR.

She wrote about how the man must have come in through an unlocked back door—*I feel so stupid for leaving it that way*—and how she awoke to find him leaning over her, cutting away her nightgown with a knife. That wasn't exactly true, but it made the story better.

The man smelled like onions, Miranda wrote, and she was sure he was there to rape her. The only question was if she would be killed.

She described reaching into the bottom drawer of her nightstand—*I was praying that my gun was there*—and finding nothing but an old can of hair spray. Which was, of course, completely useless as a weapon, unless your attacker happens to be holding a flaming cigarette lighter in front of his face.

God must have been with me, Miranda wrote. *Why else, unless He was watching, would a can of Alberto VO5 be right where I needed it?*

"Wait a minute," Ed Merritt said when he did the edit, "I thought God used Aquanet."

Miranda told of raising the can, pressing the button, and directing the spray into the flame of the cigarette lighter. Writing, *It was like having my own personal blowtorch that I aimed at my attacker's head. Instantly, his face and hair were on fire.*

"You smell the burning flesh?" Ed Merritt asked. "Just curious."

The man was screaming, Miranda wrote, *as he ran from her house, into the night.*

He's still out there, Miranda said in the story's last line. *They haven't caught him yet. But I'll bet he's more scared of me now than I am of him.*

You read this shit?" Arthur Murry Murray tossed the paper on the bare concrete floor. "First off, ain't no way I smelled like onions. Garlic, sure, 'cause I had linguini with clam sauce for dinner. At Stanley's on the beach. You been there yet?"

"No."

"And they ain't made a breath mint yet that can ace garlic." Arthur blew into his cupped palm and sniffed. Then, "Second off, my face and hair was not on fire, no way, no how. I mean, I think I would be the first to know. Only thing that caught fire was my sleeve."

Arthur picked the paper up again, read a few words, and tossed it down again. "Now, screaming while I ran outta the house . . . All right, she's got me there. Tell me you wouldn't scream, your clothes was on fire. Lucky for me I could get that jacket off, whack it on the ground a few times."

"Gonna ask you once more and that's it, Arthur. You want to shut your yap and help me with this?"

"And this bit about being scared of her? Give me a fucking break." Arthur shook his head. "Only one thing in the world that Arthur Murry Murray worries about, which we all know is water. Well, that and not having enough to eat. But not no reporter. All right, fine, she surprised me with the flamethrower. Had it to do over again, I wouldn't of flicked the Bic, wouldn't of given her any fire to work with. Hey, all's I was doing was trying to see was the bitch naked."

Reece Pepper said, "All right, that's it."

"That was good linguini with clams, though." Arthur smacked his lips. "Stanley's on the beach. You been there yet?"

Reece Pepper stood in the middle of the ten-by-ten-foot U-Stor-It unit, five miles off the interstate on the mainland side. The place catered to hunters. Each unit had its own top-loading deep-freeze, big enough for the carcass of a good-sized buck. But not, as it turned out, quite large enough for a full-length, fat-ass, small-town cop.

Right now Reece was holding a saw and thinking that of all the butt-pains in the world, working with snitches was the biggest. Especially this snitch.

He threw the saw—it had a bowed-pipe handle and was good for cutting tree limbs—against the sheet metal wall. The sound of it, like a clap of tin thunder, made Arthur jump.

"Fuck almighty." Arthur put his hand over his heart. "Thought for a second there somebody took a shot at us." He shook his head and pointed to the corpse. It lay on the floor, wrapped in a plastic tarp. "Having a fresh stiff in the room makes me nervous," Arthur said. "'Cause you never know when the putrefaction is gonna start."

"Maybe," Reece said, "we need two of them." He reached into the back of his waistband and pulled a .38 Special, then took two steps toward Arthur and put the gun barrel against his head. Saying, "On your knees."

"Not again," Arthur said. "How long we gotta do this tough-cop shit?"

Reece thumbed the hammer back. Arthur said, "All right, all right. How's about I just squat? That work?"

"You want to know how I spent last night," Reece said, "while you was slurping down your clams?"

Arthur sniffed. "That what this is about, man? You pissed 'cause I didn't invite you to dinner?"

Reece almost did it then and there, came within a hair of pulling the trigger and putting a hole in the gasbag this idiot called a head. But he thought about all the work he had put into this, and then he thought about the cash. Telling himself, Don't lose your patience and blow the whole deal. Asking himself, How often do you get a snitch who's the right-hand man of the dude you want? He relaxed his finger slightly.

"Here's what I did, Arthur, not that you care. I'm casing Flippo, right? When I see this hick cop trying to do the same thing."

"You mind I get outta this squat, man? I got a bad leg."

"Takes me about ten seconds to see the hick cop's gonna get in the way and screw up our whole deal."

"Like I said, I got this bad leg—"

"Then the dumb rube cop, with me following him, goes out to a goddamn submarine—you believing that?—in a park out in the middle of nowhere. Climbs inside the sub, and then he must of forgot something, because he comes climbing back out. I jumped in and waited for him to come back. Which he did, the dumb S.O.B."

"Got this bad leg in prison, man. You know, the medical care in there should be an embarrassment to the entire state of Texas."

"So I take care of this guy in the submarine, okay? Then I hear somebody coming, I hide, and guess who it is. It's fucking Flippo, you believe that?"

Arthur groaned. "Either shoot me or let me stand up. This thing is killing me."

"I'm thinking, Flippo's onto me, but he splits, don't ask me why. He's just flat gone. So then I gotta haul this stiff away. I mean, dead cops tend to attract attention. Ask you this, you ever pulled a mega-pound dead dude out of a submarine before? Ain't as easy as it looks."

"Hey, I stole a leather couch from a second-floor apartment once. Broad daylight, too." Arthur tried to shift his squat and fell to one knee on the dirty concrete floor. "Now look what you done, man. Brand-new pants."

Reece, feeling calmer, pulled the gun from Arthur's head. "Stand up, Arthur, help me cut this guy down to freezer size."

Arthur stood and brushed dirt from his knees. Reece retrieved his saw from where he had thrown it.

"Reminds me of a joke," Reece said.

Arthur moaned. "Oh, Jesus."

"Guy says, 'Anybody seen my dog with no legs? Oh, well, it's probably right where I left it.'"

THE GALVESTON POLICE PUT Jack in a holding
room, not exactly four-star accommodations for the ace
witness—or chief suspect, take your pick—to what
would have been the biggest murder of the year. Would
have been if only they could show it had actually happened. All they needed was a body, or some blood, or a
single piece of physical evidence pointing to the commis-
sion of a crime. They were desperate enough, they might
go with a missing persons report. Even that hadn't come
in.

If they had anything at all, Jack knew, they would be
hosing him down with questions and threats. But all they
had done was take his statement, then put him in this
room.

It was painted the color of green that you find on old
leftovers in the back of the refrigerator, and had smeared
glass windows onto the squad room. The two fluorescent
lights buzzed and blinked. A single-plank wooden bench,
mounted on upright steel pipes, ran the length of the
room. Jack tried lying on it, but every time he neared

sleep he would fall off. The third time it happened, he bedded down on the gray linoleum floor.

Around dawn the cops let him have a sausage sandwich from the vending machine and a couple of cups of coffee that tasted like yesterday's Quaker State French Roast. If my stomach had legs, Jack was thinking, it would have walked out on me by now.

Just after nine o'clock the door opened and a tall man calling himself Lieutenant Torres walked in. He wore half-frame reading glasses and looked tired in the way of cops who had seen it all but had managed not to go dead in the soul.

Lieutenant Torres sat on the bench next to Jack. "I checked you out," he said. "Made some calls, asked around. Know what people in Dallas told me about Jack Flippo?"

"That depends. You reach any of my ex-wives?"

The lieutenant showed him a weak smile, then removed his glasses. "They told me that you've done your share of stupid things—"

"Thank you, dear friends."

"—but they weren't aware of any bouts of hallucination."

Jack nodded, so tired he could barely move his head. "If I see something, it's there. If it's not, I don't."

Torres checked his watch. "We've had five officers and two dogs searching that end of the island since dawn."

"Fine," Jack said. "But this guy I saw was in no shape to crawl away and collapse in the bushes. That dude's crawling days were done."

"Found a few empty cars parked near the water," Torres said, "but they probably belong to fishermen. What was your victim driving?"

"You know, he neglected to say."

The lieutenant studied a paper he was holding. Jack read upside-down. Torres saw him doing it and turned the paper his way. "Want to see it? It's your statement to the detectives."

"Not really."

"Maybe you have something to add. Now that you've had time to think."

Jack rubbed his eyes and shook his head. "Nope."

"Says here you jumped the fence to get in and out."

"Still spry for my age."

"Didn't cut the fence, that's interesting." Torres seemed to be pondering something. Then, "Odd time and place to meet a client."

"Tell me about it."

"Drug dealer, sure. But a client?"

Jack sat up straight and returned Torres's stare. "My guess is, while I've been cooling on the bench here, your boys searched my car and my room."

"We got a warrant."

"I'm sure you did. So tell me what drugs you found."

The lieutenant cleared his throat. "What seems a little hard to swallow? That you don't know this client's name."

"If I were you, I might think the same thing." Jack took a deep breath and let it out. "So. Are we done here?"

The lieutenant gave him a long stare, then sighed and left the room. After six hours in custody, Jack walked out of the police station with a misdemeanor citation for trespassing.

Miranda watched Ed Merritt approach from across the room. The guy walked like someone with no testicles, like a man with absolutely nothing down there in the package except a little tube to pee with. She waited for him to arrive, then pounced.

"You've seen what I can really do," she said, "so now I'll hop on this jail escape story."

Ed Merritt sat on the corner of her desk and smiled. Bad news, his blandola grin was back. "Got a good one for you," he said.

"Jesus H." Miranda picked up the A section and pointed to her story. "Did you happen to see my piece, Ed? My first-person brush with fucking death? Readers have been calling me all day. I've got women phoning me in tears. Tears, Ed, I'm bringing tears to readers' eyes. So could you just once let me run with a story that looks good to me, instead of this drivel you keep puking up?"

She was talking so loud that everyone in the room had turned to look.

Ed Merritt blinked a few times but kept smiling. He said, "Drivel and puke, that's a mixed metaphor. Anyway, got a nice little feature for you about a lady astrologer who has twelve pet ducks, each one named for a sign of the zodiac. Could be page one."

He walked away. Miranda wished she had a gun.

Her phone was ringing. The caller, a woman, wanted to talk about the escaped lawyer. "You know what?" Miranda said. "These assholes here don't care about that story, so why should I? Call Jack Flippo at the Driftwood Motel." She slammed down the phone.

A minute later Miranda slumped at her desk and said to no one in particular, "Now, why the fuck did I do that?"

Back at his motel, Jack cleaned up quickly and went in search of an afternoon breakfast, the best kind. If every meal was breakfast it would be all right with him. But maybe, just for today, no hair of the dog; he would stay out of Theo's.

Nice day, so he decided to walk. He strolled down Seawall, the gulf glistening to his left, thunderheads starting to build in the distance beyond the bayside. Happy, laughing tourists passed him on bicycles and Rollerblades. He enjoyed hearing them laugh. Jack had that sunny, floating-free outlook on life that you get when you walk out of jail. In his experience, it usually lasted about an hour.

For the first time in days, his muscles didn't seem to be made of chicken feathers and old glue. His head was clear—clear enough, at least, for him to see that he couldn't make sense of anything that had happened this week.

And he was alert enough to tell that someone was following him: a black pickup truck with tinted windows, hanging back about fifty yards, going so slow that the other traffic had to pull around it. Might have been the worst tail job Jack had ever seen.

He passed the San Luis Hotel with the truck still back there, then saw in the next block, as if he had planned it, a pancake house. Jack went inside and got a booth, watching through the plate glass as the black pickup pulled into the lot. Two minutes later, as Jack studied the menu, someone slid into the seat across the table from him with, "Mind if I join you?"

Jack looked up and said, "You're in luck. Escaped prisoners eat for half-price on Tuesdays."

"Man." Wesley Joy wiped his forehead with a napkin. "This boy has been sitting outside that motel of yours for a couple of hours, waiting for you to show. Let me say this: It gets a little warm in that truck with the windows rolled up. Another half hour, you coulda stuck an apple in my mouth and served me at the luau."

"Roll the windows down, then."

"Easy for you to say. They ain't tacking your picture up in the post office, next to the real criminals."

Jack nodded. "You're trying to stay out of sight. I understand. So maybe a crowded restaurant isn't the best place for someone like you."

Wesley pulled his Houston Astros cap a little lower and pushed his dark glasses up his nose. His hands were trembly and had liver spots. He said, "It's okay, because you weren't followed. That's what old Wesley was watching for. . . . So, you ready to talk? Ready to get us a plan?"

Jack sipped coffee. Then, "What did you do last night?"

"Watched *Hollywood Squares* and practiced self-abuse like a teenager. Ain't nobody gets me hard the way Whoopi Goldberg does."

Jack waited.

"What the hell you think I did, Jack?" Wesley dropped his head and lowered his voice. "I got in that truck you see out there, and I drove to every dock, pier, and marina I could find in Galveston. Looking for Angelique and her boat. I mean, that's pretty much my mission in life right now, case you hadn't noticed."

"What about going to the submarine?"

Wesley slipped the sunglasses down the bridge of his nose and peered over the rim with his one good eye. "You're telling me the bitch has got herself a submarine now?"

Jack rubbed his eye and got a flash of B. T. Mack with the rope around his neck. "You through with the smart-ass?"

"Hey, you're the one who brought it up."

"Let's try this again."

"Make it fast. That busboy's starting to look at me funny."

Jack leaned forward on his elbows. "Last night, while I was sitting in a greasy spoon, I got a message from you—"

"In a what? Nuh-uh." Wesley shook his head. "Not from me. Not last night."

"—that said to meet you on Pelican Island."

"Never heard of it."

Jack's voice was near a whisper. "I get to Pelican Island, and what do you think I find?"

"Wild guess, I'd say pelicans."

"I find a Luster, Texas, police officer."

"Oh, shit, they're closing in, Jack."

"Not this one. This one was dead."

They stared at each other, the pancake house clattering around them. Finally Wesley said, "Time for the truth now, Jack. This is a moment demanding honest candor."

"Absolutely."

"Time to lay all the cards on the table."

"I'm with you, Wesley."

"So let old Wesley just get it right out in the open, right here, right now."

"I'm ready."

Wesley took a deep breath. Then, "Jackie, did you kill that cop?"

"What? Hell no, I didn't kill him. I want to know if you did."

"Me? Why would I want to kill a cop from Luster? I'm innocent, Jackie, remember? I mean, look at me."

Jack wondered how you read the face of a one-eyed man wearing dark glasses.

"You do remember?" Wesley said.

"Here's the strange part." Jack waited while the waitress warmed his coffee. When she was gone he said, "After I found the body, I left the submarine to call the cops. Had to come back into Galveston to do it. By the time we all got back out to Pelican Island, the body was gone."

"Gone where?"

"That's a good question."

Wesley sat back and folded his arms. "The boy wasn't really dead, then."

"Yes, he was."

"Playing possum, maybe. Then, after you took off, so did he."

Jack rubbed his chin, thinking it over. "My guess is, the killer carted him off."

"You take his pulse? Maybe he was just low sick."

"No way."

"Hey, it happens all the time, even to the professionals. People get pronounced dead by the coroner, next thing you know, they wake up in the morgue with a tag on their toe."

"That's not what happened here."

"Sometimes, Jackie, a mortal will pass to the other side, but the good Lord kicks their ass back where they came from. Tells them they're not ready yet. They see a white light, but that's all they see. I believe that."

"Fine." Jack wasn't in the mood to argue. He changed the subject. "You know a federal narc named Reece Pepper?"

Wesley froze. "Everybody in southeast Texas knows Reece Pepper. Why?"

"Number one, he's here in Galveston looking for you."

"Please tell me that ain't so."

"Number two," Jack said, "something about this whole thing has his smell on it. I can't tell you why exactly." He shook his head. "Just a hunch."

"Oh, man." Wesley looked around the room again. "I don't understand why Reece Pepper'd be in Galveston."

"Like I said, looking for you. Last time I checked, Wesley, you were the suspect in a big drug murder. So it makes sense that a federal narc would show up."

"You talked to R.C.?" Wesley said.

"Who?"

"I mean Reece. You talk to him."

"Sure."

"What'd he tell you?"

Jack planned to give Wesley the whole truth, just not quite yet. "Other than he wants to know where you are? He told me a joke about lawyers and Viagra."

"Lord have mercy, this is some shitty week." Wesley rubbed the back of his neck. "Jail escape, federal narc on my ass, and now a dead cop, maybe."

"I'd say we need to get to work."

"They'll try to pin that cop killing on me, too. You know they will."

"Maybe. If the body ever turns up."

Wesley put his face in his hands. "How in the world, Jackie, did it come to this? What did this old boy do to deserve such a fate?"

Jack could have given him a Calvinist sermon, or some gibberish about karma, or a simple lecture on cause and effect. Instead he said, "Sometimes the cards just come up bad."

"When Angelique and I left Dallas? And came down here for the joys of semi-retirement? All old Wesley wanted was to relax by the ocean, to smell the salt air every morning, watch the waves break gently over the sand. The simple pleasures, Jackie, that's all. Plus cash flow and pussy, of course."

"Goes without saying." Jack cleared his throat. "Listen, Wesley—"

"I mean, is that too much for one man to ask?" Wesley cut loose with a heavy sigh. "You know, I probably sealed my fate the day I filed divorce papers."

Jack stared. "What did you say?"

"Me and Angelique? That marriage ran outta gas about the time we hit Galveston. Now she's one judge's signature away from becoming the former Mrs. Joy number five. And I got one thing to say about that: Thank God there's no alimony in Texas."

Jack looked past him, through the window and toward the Gulf: water as far as you could see. He said, "Angelique."

"That's why she's letting me dangle, Jackie, why she hasn't come forward yet. That's what women do to you when they're pissed off, my friend, don't know if you've noticed. She wants Wesley to suffer. You see that, don't you?"

Jack wasn't really listening now. He had heard everything he needed to hear. He waited for Wesley to stop talking, then said, "All right, the cops must know you're here somewhere. You need to get your ass to your safe house, or your fleabag joint, wherever, and stay there."

Wesley nodded. "You got the right idea."

"Where is it?" He watched as Wesley wrote an address and phone number on a napkin and slid it to him.

"Good," Jack said. "Now, you lay low. I'll find Angelique."

Wesley drove back to the Tweety Motel, thinking about Reece Pepper all the way. Telling himself, in Galveston? This was giving off the smell of a double-screw.

He would like to ask Arthur what had happened to their simple plan, to their foolproof feint. As he drove he did the step-by-step in his head, as if he were looking for a short in the wiring. The way it was supposed to have worked: As soon as Wesley broke jail, Arthur was to phone Daryl Dee Bird. Daryl Dee, an old cellmate of Arthur's, was one of Reece's ace operatives. A smear of slime, Daryl Dee, but at least you could count on him to relay info.

Arthur was supposed to tell Daryl Dee one thing, which was that Wesley had gone to ground in Dallas. That's all, just enough to get Reece Pepper out of the picture for a few days, three hundred miles away in Big D with his thumb up his ass, looking for Wesley.

So somehow it had broken down. Such things happened. In nearly every criminal case that Wesley had taken to trial over the years, the motor had sputtered at one point or another. Witnesses flaked, stories got changed, evidence disappeared. Nothing ever went exactly as planned.

Usually he had been able to blame bad breaks or faulty machinery. But two or three times he had simply been the victim of betrayal. Each time, it had happened because Wesley forgot the rule that applied both to street fighting and trying a case: Watch your back.

When he reached the Tweety, Wesley circled the parking lot twice, on the prowl for stakeouts. Then he went to his room, where he found Arthur sitting on the bed, watching TV and eating Kraft caramels.

"Speak of the devil," Wesley said. "Where've you been the last twelve hours or so?"

"Felt like waxing the weasel."

Wesley nodded. "Seems like that sort of activity maybe could wait till we're done here. This being my life and freedom on the line."

"Easy for you to say." Caramel-colored saliva dribbled down Arthur's chin. "You, a guy who spent, what, two weeks in jail? Poor baby. Try three years poozle-free, then see if you're not taking all your orders from Captain Dick and the Two Nut Brothers."

Wesley gave it a couple of minutes. Thinking that the odd thing about rats, about the ones who had sold you out, was how often they let you know what they had done. It was always a little something: an odd phrase they dropped, or a snatch of knowledge they shouldn't have had, or the flashing of a matchbook from someplace they shouldn't have been. Their betrayal became like a worm within them that had to work its way outward. Sooner or later, without knowing it, they revealed themselves.

Finally Wesley said, "I think we're damn close to wrapping this whole thing up."

Arthur nodded, still annoyed. "What I'm telling you is, try three years gash-deprived, see if the purple-helmeted warrior of love ain't calling all your shots."

"Probably right. Listen, I just talked to brother Flippo—"

"Hey, the asshole sent me to prison, remember. So he ain't no brother of mine."

"Fine. The point is, the wheels may be turning at last."

"What kinda wheels?" Arthur said.

"The wheels that take us to where we need to be."

Arthur laughed at something on TV. Then said to Wesley, "I got a good one for you. You want to hear it?"

"Not really," Wesley said.

"Come on, you'll laugh your ass off." Arthur crammed four or five caramels into his mouth but kept talking. "Know what happens"—he belched—"when you give Viagra to a lawyer?"

Jack couldn't remember the last time he had been so tired. He unlocked the door to this room at the Driftwood and went straight for the bed, thinking that he would lie down for just a few minutes.

He checked the clock—almost four. Then he closed his eyes and felt himself drift like a rose petal dropped into a well.

Sometime later—it seemed like five minutes, but the clock said two hours—he awoke. The room was near dark. For a moment, as he blinked and struggled to sit up, he couldn't remember where he was. But soon it came to him: He was in a cheap motel with a storm blowing outside.

Jack leaned his back against the wall and listened to the rain beating against the window. Thunder boomed and the flimsy building shook. Something must have broken loose in the wind; it hit the door with a double rap. A few seconds later, and there it was again. That's when Jack realized someone was knocking.

He rose from the bed and opened the door. A woman stood in the howl of the storm, drenched, with a half smile on her face, looking like the wet-dream delivery service. It was Angelique Joy.

THE FIRST TIME EVER that Jack saw Angelique, she threw a carving knife at her husband. Jack liked her right away.

That was two years ago. Wesley had brought Jack home after the two of them had drunk so much bourbon they began to weep. They had started sipping Old Grandad at sundown, corner table at the Tradewinds in Dallas, and were still at it around midnight. Wesley had passed out about nine o'clock, but he revived an hour later. He lifted his head and began screaming, "Christ in the manger, I've gone blind!"

Jack raised his hands toward the ceiling, shouting, "Heal this sinner." Then he reached across the table and repositioned Wesley's eye patch. It had shifted from his bad eye to his good one while he had been facedown on the table.

After everything settled down and a new round of drinks was served, Wesley began to talk about his father. Tears rolled down his face. "You know, he died broke and brokenhearted," Wesley said. "Just a poor old busted-down man."

"Eats you up, doesn't it?" Jack said.

"Know this: After his Filipino mail-order bride took off with a long-haul trucker, he didn't have the will to go on. And can you blame him?"

"Oh, man. His wife left him?" Jack said.

Wesley nodded. "All because he wouldn't get cable. Know what the damn trucker told her? Said every motel *he* stayed at had free HBO. Daddy just couldn't compete with that."

"Both my wives left me. Number two went just last week."

"A poor old busted-down man, Jack. And I'll swear to you right now, old Wesley will never, ever end up that way. Not like Daddy, nuh-uh."

"Just walked out the door, both of them." Jack shook his head. "Wasn't their fault, though."

Wesley backhanded the air. "Don't get me started on the women and what they do to you. Listen, my second ex? She had this old boy actually going along for the grocery shopping. Had me down at the Tom Thumb squeezing canteloupes, Jackie, like some kind of girly man."

"If it was anybody's fault that they left, it was mine."

"Full disclosure, though. Every time I went shopping with her? We'd get home, she'd give me oral pleasure."

Jack stared into his ice cubes. "This last one, I don't know . . . I never knew a house could feel that empty."

"You think I'm bullshitting, don't you? You think old Wesley is laying on the crap." He stroked his mustache. "I'm telling you she did it every time, right there in the kitchen, but only after we got the ice cream put away."

"Know what I wish? That somebody'd just back a big truck up to the house and carry everything in there away. Clothes, furniture, old magazines, all of it. Just wipe the slate clean."

"Now, after a woman does that to you a few times, you get to anticipating the payoff. So usually, by the time we got to the dairy section, old Wesley was in full, long–may–it–wave arousal." He looked away dreamily. "Put me under oath, Jackie, I'd have to say wife number two was the best of the bunch. But oh, my God, how she busted my balls in property settlement."

"Property settlement." Jack emptied his glass, and cocktail number eight was history. "That's the meanest damn term in the law books, you know it?"

"It's right up there," Wesley said, "though I believe I'd give the nod to lethal injection."

"I mean, who cares about the property when your soul's breaking apart on the rocks?"

"Well, that's real poetic and all." Wesley cleared his throat. "But the bitch tried to take my new Jaguar convertible, Jack. And this was after she already got the house."

Jack stared toward the far wall of the Tradewinds, in the direction of the fifty-cent pool tables. He saw an old man in a straw cowboy hat playing eight ball, and it was like catching sight of himself thirty years from now: alone—no surprise there—but worse than that, old and alone with nothing worth looking back on.

"What have I ever done for anyone?" Jack said. "Nothing, that's what."

"That's not true, Jackie. You bought the last round."

"Life ought to be like a garden, don't you think? Plant flowers, you know it? Roses, man. Daffodils. And what's the purple one"— Jack tried to snap his fingers —"smells like grandma's perfume?"

"Here we go with the poetry again. My advice is, that gets you nothing but trouble."

"My garden? Shit. My garden's not even a patch of weeds."

"Sure it is," Wesley said. "You got plenty of weeds. You got weeds out the ass, Jackie."

Now Jack was crying, or close to it.

"My friend," Wesley said, "you're in some kind of bad shape. You're like four flat tires on a rainy night." He put an arm around Jack's shoulders. "Let's get you out of here, go on over to the shack."

Jack drove. Somehow they made their way to Wesley's house without killing anyone. It was a seven-mile trip, and they sang "Woolly Bully" together the whole way.

"Step on inside," Wesley said as he managed to unlock his front door, "see if the old lady won't fix us a midnight snack."

Jack came into the house and got directions to a bathroom off the hall. He stepped in and closed the bathroom door. There were monogrammed hand towels hanging on brass-plated rings next to the sink. Jack stared at them for a while, and at the pink oval rug on the floor, and then at the dried flowers in a vase atop the toilet tank. Evidence, he told himself, of the heartbreaking female touch. He later found out it was actually evidence of a Neiman Marcus decorator's touch.

As he pissed, Jack heard Wesley yelling for his wife, and soon a woman's voice was yelling back. When he emerged from the bathroom, Jack found Wesley slumped on a brown leather couch in the living room.

"Here he is," Wesley announced, "my damn good friend. Thought we'd lost you." He boomed toward the kitchen, "My friend who needs a sandwich! Right now, goddamnit!"

"Don't need any sandwiches," Jack muttered, sinking into a chair.

"A ham sandwich on toast," Wesley called. "Got that?" He shook his head. "She's a good-looking woman, Jackie, but mean as a damn wolverine. And lazy? Oh, my God."

A woman came around the corner and into the room. "I heard that," she said.

Jack looked her over, which wasn't hard with the nightgown she was wearing, like something off the cover of *True Detective*. She was blonde, early thirties, built for show: what every guy in his fifties looked for in a fifth wife.

In one hand she held a plate with a small ham on it. In the other she had a twelve-inch carving knife. "I said I heard what you said," she told Wesley.

Wesley wasn't answering. He had sunk deeper into the couch and closed his eye. Jack couldn't be sure, but he thought Wesley might be snoring.

From ten feet away, the woman heaved the plate in Wesley's direction. It hit the floor at his feet.

The plate shattered. The ham rolled across the Persian carpet and came to rest against the leg of a coffee table.

"Maybe I should be going," Jack said.

Now she held only the knife. She transferred it to her right hand, holding the blade between thumb and forefinger. She raised it above her shoulder.

"Oh, no," Jack said, "don't do that."

She had a look in her eyes that made Jack think of kerosene at the moment a match hits it.

"Better put that down," he said, "before you hurt someone."

She threw it. The knife flew end over end and struck the couch cushion between Wesley's legs, a few inches south of his crotch. It was buried to the handle.

"Whoa," Jack said. "You could work in my circus anytime."

The woman appeared surprised at herself, staring at her throwing hand. Then, just for a second or two, a smile flickered across her face.

Wesley stirred and awakened. Glancing around and asking, "Now, where was I?" He pulled the knife from the cushion, as if he had expected it to be there all along. Then he knelt on the floor and picked the ham up off the rug.

"Fine," he said as he wiped couch padding off the blade. "I'll slice it myself."

Never mind all the drunken moaning about what he should have been. That was a time, Jack thought now, when he was able to see himself as he really was. It wasn't a pretty period, but it did have its moments of pleasure.

Jack remembered it all as he reentered his room at the Driftwood Motel. Angelique, who had come in from the storm shivering, had gone into the bathroom to change. Jack had given her some pajamas, then taken her wet clothes to a coin-op dryer in a little room just off the Driftwood swimming pool.

The shower came on with a squeak of the faucets. He closed his eyes and listened to the water beat against the plastic curtain.

Jack lay on his bed at the Driftwood and remembered how Wesley had suggested, after they ate their ham-with-carpet-lint sandwiches, that Jack stay with him and Angelique for a while. Just a few days, Wesley said, telling Angelique about Jack's wife leaving him, saying that it might be good for him to be around some people for a night or two. Jack had surprised himself by saying yes.

A night or two turned into three and a half weeks. He stayed in the guest bedroom, which the Neiman-Marcus decorator had furnished in lacquered white with gilt accents, and big paintings of sad-eyed angels in stainless-steel frames, like the modern corporate headquarters of a whorehouse franchise.

When he wasn't out working, Jack spent most of the time in the bedroom, watching old movies on TV. He was licking his broken-marriage wounds and vowing to live his life the way he should, all while enjoying Wesley's hospitality in ways his old friend probably hadn't intended.

It was the same old pattern for Jack: promising better but delivering worse.

Now, at the Driftwood, the bathroom door opened. Steam billowed out, and Angelique emerged wearing Jack's red plaid pajamas. The shirt was unbuttoned, one breast showing.

She raised the fabric to her face and breathed in. "This smells like you," she said. "I remember that smell. Do you still taste the same, too?"

"One way to find out," he said.

They fell to the bed together and began to undress each other, buttons popping. Then, no prelims, straight to the main event. Angelique was on top, digging her nails into Jack's chest. About the time she drew blood,

Jack flipped her over and stretched her out, pinning her wrists and ankles to the bed. The sounds from Angelique when she came always made Jack think of whooping cranes.

This was the way they had done it dozens of times in the guest bedroom at Angelique's house in Dallas, with the pictures of sad-eyed angels looking on. The chief difference now was that Wesley wasn't asleep just down the hall.

Early dark, thanks to the storm, streetlights blinking on. Wesley and Arthur Murry Murray drove down Seawall Boulevard, Arthur's truck. The gray Gulf lay on their left, with the roadway flooding: six inches of water from curb to curb. The car raised a spray from each fender as it plowed through.

"No sir, this boy does not like the water," Arthur said. "I mention that?"

"Couple of times, maybe." Wesley nodded. "Seven or eight. Enough."

"Bad enough in this place you gotta look at the ocean full of water all the time," Arthur cranked the windshield wipers to full speed. "On top of that it comes pouring from the sky, too. When this is all over? When you and me nail this down? I'm taking my stake and moving someplace you don't have to look at water."

"I'm guessing, then, that Venice is out."

"Was a time Vegas would be my first choice. But you seen that place lately?"

"The last time I was in Las Vegas," Wesley said, "I caught 'Nudes on Ice' at the Union Plaza. That, friends, is entertainment."

"All of a sudden they got water everywhere in Vegas. Drive down the Strip, big fountains is all you see. One joint, swear on a Bible, they got a fucking lake with a fucking pirate ship. And the swimming pools, oh my God." Arthur sniffed. "So Vegas is off the list. I'm thinking Utah now."

"You and the Mormons," Wesley said. "A perfect fit."

"High and dry is where I want to be. Clear blue skies and solid earth. Once I leave this shithole island? Don't never want to see one more swimming pool."

"Fine. We can arrange that." Wesley cleared his throat. "Now, to the business at hand. You say we can get in the back way with nobody seeing us."

"Worked the last time."

"Ten more minutes, it'll be nice and dark. With nobody in the house, we'll make it quick."

"Whatever you say, big boss." Arthur ran a couple of fingers across his scorched eyebrow stubble. "But I gotta tell you this don't seem like a choice idea to me."

Wesley turned toward him. "Arthur, you going south on me now?"

Arthur shook his head. "This boy don't go south."

"You gonna run to Mommy now?"

"It's just . . . the cops, you know, I—"

"Who's the damn fugitive in this car, anyway?"

Arthur sighed. "You are."

"Who's got the warrant for his arrest?"

Arthur, quietly: "You do."

"Who's gotta find his cunt-o-rama of a wife before he can walk the streets a free man?"

"I get the point."

"I don't think you do." Wesley smoothed his silver mustache. "So let me repeat myself. As I told you, I have a present to deliver. And a message for anyone who feels like paying attention."

"Message? Shit, Wesley, that's why they got mailmen."

"This one needs a special kind of home delivery. Call it the personal touch."

When they were done, they lay in the Driftwood bed, both on their backs. Angelique closed her eyes. Jack stared at brown stains on the ceiling tiles. Neither of them said anything for fifteen minutes or so. Finally Angelique came out with, "Know what I always liked about you?"

"I'm guessing it's a toss-up between my wealth and my savoir faire."

"I always liked," she said, "the way you couldn't get enough of me."

That was true. When he was staying at Wesley's house, Jack would sit behind the closed bedroom door at night, like a dog waiting to be fed. If he'd had a tail, he would have been wagging it. Around eleven o'clock, he would hear the creak of footsteps in the hallway, followed by a light knock. The door would open, and there would be Angelique in one of her nightgowns. The woman had some nightgowns.

She usually stayed for a couple of hours, maybe three if they managed to screw twice. Then, back to Wesley's bed. In the morning they would all have breakfast together—with Wesley talking sports through a hangover—and go off to work.

"Same now as it was then," Jack said. He ran two fingers from her hip toward what his college roommate used to call the mysterious triangular forest of Poonagonia. "Like the song says, you're the whip and I'm the cream."

"That day in the Adolphus Hotel?" Angelique said. "Hardest thing I ever did, walking away from you."

"Fanciest place I've ever been dumped in, the Adolphus." Jack kept his finger working. "But it would have been nice, maybe, to know the reason you bailed, instead of leaving it to my imagination. My imagination's a bad place to leave anything."

"I told you." She reached down and placed two of her fingers on top of Jack's, total of four in the wet now. "I told you all of it, then and there."

"You said, your exact words, that you had fallen in love with the wrong man."

"Right." She moaned. "I did. At first sight."

He waited while her fingers and his worked together. The whooping crane was back in the room, though not as loud as before. When she was done Angelique said, "Any more of that and I'll need crutches."

Jack waited. "Now that I've got you, who was that wrong man?"

She turned toward Jack and blinked twice, slowly. "Are you serious?"

"You know me. Always asking questions."

Angelique sighed and shook her head. "God, why do I always pick the dumb ones?" Then to Jack, "I was talking about you."

"Say what?"

"You didn't know?"

"Why the hell didn't you tell me?"

"I *did* tell you."

Jack felt for a moment as if the floor were moving. "Whatever happened to the old-fashioned way, to plain old I love you? The direct approach."

"Somebody tells you they love you, and you complain about the way it was said?" She rolled out of bed and walked to the far side of the room. "Jesus, maybe I take it all back."

She turned, and they stared at each other. Angelique had brown eyes with blades of yellow. Jack sat up and ran his gaze down her body. Every other encounter had come in a dark room; this was the first time he had ever seen her naked with the lights on. It looked as good as it felt.

He swallowed and said, "So you told me that you loved me, then ran off with your husband."

"That's right."

"I thought it was supposed to work the other way around."

Angelique moved toward him with her arms out. That look on her face, man. Jack readied himself for a kiss or a hug, or maybe even a return favor for the finger exercise. Thinking that there were worse things to have coming at you than an unclothed woman.

She stopped a foot from him, smiled, drew her arm back and punched him just below his chest.

Her fist caught him in the soft pit under the center of his ribs. Air flew out of him, and he wasn't sure when it was coming back.

"At least I didn't kick you in the balls," she said.

Jack gasped, "Because you love me."

"That's right."

Angelique pulled the pajamas back on while Jack found his breath. "Just out of curiosity," he finally managed to say, "why'd you do that?"

"For being stupid," she said.

"You can get beat up for that? This is bad news."

"That day . . ." Angelique sat on the edge of the mattress. The bed sagged; so did she. "That day I walked away from you . . ."

"Also known as the day I watched you go."

"Exactly. You watched me." She stood again. Jack wondered if he was about to take another punch. "All you had to do," she said, "was ask me to stay."

"You're kidding," he said. You're lying, he thought.

"One word would have done it. 'Stop.' 'Wait.' Any of those."

He looked at her, and she looked at him. With Jack thinking that Angelique was one of those women who cut through your life like a small but lethal springtime tornado, whipping this way and that. Destroying your head but keeping your heart, the way the twisters would demolish half the house yet leave a glass of milk untouched on the kitchen table.

"And because I failed to say anything," Jack said, "you and Wesley left town."

"Pretty much, yeah. We talked it over, thought a change of scene might help us patch the marriage up." She ran fingers through her hair. "It didn't."

Jack recalled the scattered reports he had picked up on Wesley after the move to Galveston: Wesley, everyone said, was avoiding friends, cutting off ex-colleagues, and running a law practice devoted to comforting the gravely afflicted dope dealers of southeast Texas.

"Word was," Jack said, "that you two were getting rich down here."

"Wesley made a lot of money, if that's what you mean." Angelique stood before the mirror, checking her hips. "Enough for a down payment on the boat. The rest of it he pissed away playing blackjack in Louisiana."

Jack watched her watch herself. He said, "Okay, money problems."

"But that's not what killed the marriage." Angelique turned to face Jack. "The killer was me and you. Wesley never got over that."

"Wait a minute—"

"Every time we had a fight, he'd dredge it up."

"He *knew*?"

"Jack, the man's not blind in both his eyes. And his ears work."

"Oh, Christ." Jack put one hand to the side of his head. "He heard us? While we were doing it?"

"Are you kidding? Nothing wakes Wesley up."

"Something to be thankful for."

"He heard it," she said, "when I told him."

They looked at each other again. "Told him"—Jack took a breath180—"how much?"

"Jack, when I decide to do something, I don't do it halfway."

"We've established that."

"He asked for details; I delivered. I even let him read my diary. That was fun."

"Don't tell me you wrote it all down."

"Oh, yeah." She settled on the bed next to him and rubbed his thigh. "Made me kind of hot, actually, giving Wesley the lowdown. Plus, I added a couple of inches to your manhood, for effect. I told him you were hung like Mr. Ed."

Jack gazed at the floor, both hands to his head now. All the winks and finger-guns from Wesley were taking on a different meaning. "I can't believe this," Jack said.

"Hey, come on." She stood again. "It's not like Wesley was Mister Pure. The boy was screwing everything but the crack of dawn. So don't get all conscience-stricken."

Jack looked up at her. "The lesser rat rationale."

"Exactly. So, to finish the story: We got down here, bought a boat, and decided we didn't have much use for each other. As man and wife, I mean. Then Wesley landed his butt in jail, and here we are." She smiled.

Jack was thinking this version was a little too condensed for him. "When I went to see Wesley in jail," he said, "he told me he only wanted one thing. For me to find you."

"Congratulations, you did it." She spread her arms. "Now what you gonna do with me? Besides what you already did, I mean."

"He wanted you." Jack waited to see if she would jump in. Then, "But I'll take a wild guess and say you're not all that eager for him"

"Never. Ever."

"And why would that be?"

She waved one hand. "There's only one thing I want from him."

"What's that?"

"He didn't tell you? What a surprise."

Jack was about to ask another question when Angelique grabbed a handful of his shirt and pulled him to
her. "Ever thought of running away on a boat?" she said.
"Just pointing it toward the sun and seeing where you
end up?"

"You're in prime middle-aged-man fantasy territory
now."

"You and me, babe, soon as we take care of business
here. Nothing to it but to do it."

"Simple as that, huh? Wesley delivers on this obliga-
tion, whatever it is, and its ahoy-matey time for you and
me."

"I'm thinking we hug the coast all the way down to
Key West," Angelique said. "Then maybe over to the
Bahamas, hit the casinos."

Jack had a vision of blue water and coconuts, could
almost hear a steel-drum band playing. He said, "What
about your testimony? To clear him."

She turned away, looking more annoyed than someone
who was about to sail to the Bahamas should. "Is that
what he told you? Testimony to clear him? Is that what
Wesley said? He's such a goddamn liar."

Jack cleared his throat. "That's why he wanted me to
find you—"

"Oh, boy, that's rich."

"—so you could take the stand and swear he didn't kill
those drug dealers."

Angelique threw out something that wasn't quite a laugh. Maybe the wrapper the laugh came in. She said, "Don't I wish it was that easy."

Jack motioned for her to sit. "Why don't you explain it all to me?"

She shook her head. "Here's the two things you need to know to make you and me happy. Number one, Wesley killed those two drug dealers."

Like a smack in the face. Jack stared. "How do you know?"

"Baby, I was sitting in the car outside the motel."

"Wait—"

"I *know* what happened. I was at the scene. I saw it all through an open door. That's why I took off."

"Hold on—"

"*That's* the testimony he's talking about. *That's* why he wants to find me."

"Man. This is too much." Jack pressed a hand to his face. "Wesley . . . Two people dead."

"You know what, I don't care. Those two greasies deserved what they got, far as I'm concerned."

"He could be looking at capital murder."

"Uh-uh." She wagged a finger. "The number-two thing you need to know: I don't want to send my soon-to-be ex-husband to death row, even if he is a shit. If Wesley wants me to disappear, I'm happy to." She stroked his arm. "You and me, Jack, we'll disappear together. But I need money to do it. That boat doesn't sail for free.

That's why we need to tell Wesley it's gonna cost two hundred thousand dollars for this girl to float away."

Jack shook his head. "Wesley said he's broke."

"Another lie. He stole that money from the drug dealers."

Reece Pepper had told him the same thing. Jack said, "How do you know this?"

"Word gets around," she said.

Jack was seeing the world in a new way.

"The main thing right now," she said, "is to get that cash from him to me." Angelique cocked her head. "Maybe you could be, like, the delivery boy."

This is it?" Wesley said.

"Be the spot." Arthur put the car in park. "Hey, you hungry?"

"Let's give it a couple minutes before we go in." Wesley turned and gazed out the rear window. "Wait till it gets to full dark, just to be sure."

"Wanna grab some Italian once we finish up here?"

"Why not . . . All right, we go through the back gate." Wesley pointed. "You sure it's not locked?"

"What if it is?" Arthur pointed to a toolbox in the bed of the truck. "I got what we need. So . . . ?"

Wesley reached into his pocket and wrapped his fingers around the gun he had stolen when he broke jail. "Sure," he said. "If you still feel like eating when we're done here."

Jack got dressed and went outside, walking to the dryer to retrieve Angelique's clothes. It was night, with the rain still falling, but gently now, a whimper after the big blow.

He worked to get more answers out of Angelique, but it was like trying to open a window that had been painted shut. He remembered cases he had worked as an assistant D.A.; no matter how neatly everything seemed to fit, there were always ragged edges. You could always find something to question.

Back in the room, Jack put the folded clothes on a chair. Angelique pulled the pajamas off and stretched, what a sight: golden tan all over. No need for bathing suits, Jack thought, out on the open sea. Out there, you could do what you wanted.

"I gotta pee," she announced and was gone behind the closed door. Jack sat on the bed. He saw her purse on the nightstand, reached for it, paused, then picked it up. Telling himself, You just can't stand it, can you?

Jack's curse: He could never quit poking. When someone handed him a gift, he wanted to know what the giver wanted. Open curtains were an invitation to gaze; closed curtains a reason to pry. Locks were for picking. The sign that said no admittance meant, to him, come on in. Jack felt driven to peep into the back alleys and hidden rooms of everyone's life but his own.

To him, a smile was like the painting that concealed a safe in the wall. If something looked good, that usually meant he hadn't looked hard enough. He was the kind of guy, an old girlfriend once told him, who would drain the lake to see what kind of fish were in it.

Some mornings that was the only thing that got him out of bed.

He cracked open Angelique's purse, finding a wallet and a key ring and a receipt from the day before for five quarts of motor oil. It came from the Tiki Island marina; now he knew where he might find her next time he was looking.

Behind that he found another piece of paper: a month-old receipt from the AAAA Bail Bond Agency of Galveston, $3,000 cash bond posted by Angelique for someone named Royal Curley, arrested for misdemeanor assault. The name meant nothing to him.

But he slipped the bond receipt under his mattress anyway, then put the purse back on the nightstand just as the bathroom door opened.

Angelique went to the desk and pulled some Driftwood Motel stationery from the drawer. Asking, "Will you talk to Wesley soon?"

"Soon as I can."

"Tell him what it will take." She was drawing a map. "Then you can bring it to me." She handed him the paper. "Sundown tomorrow."

"And then what?"

"And then," she said, "we cruise away."

Jack nodded. "Sails whipping in the breeze, blue water, Key West at sunset. Beats anything I've got back in Dallas. Which isn't that hard to do, you think about it."

"I can't wait." She stood before the mirror, her back to him, brushing her hair. "It's gonna be better than you can imagine."

"You bet." Jack rubbed the stubble on his chin. "But I just have this feeling—a little nagging thing—that there's a few bumps in the road between now and bliss."

"Funny you should mention that," Angelique said. "I meant to tell you this on the way in. You do know, don't you, that you're being watched?"

14

FINALLY THE RAIN HAD stopped. It was coming down dogs and sausages for a while—so hard that Reece Pepper couldn't make the face of the woman who had come to the door of room 119, Driftwood Motel. He had been thirty yards away, tops, so he should have been able to see her clearly. But it was like monsoon night in Samboville out there.

She had been in the room for almost an hour at this point. Long enough for Flippo to hustle her wet clothes to the laundry room and then go back and get them later. And what, Reece wondered, was the lady wearing in the meantime?

So Reece sat in his car, feeling his ass widen and his piles throb, looking through a pair of high-powered U.S. government binoculars. Five hundred bucks apiece these babies cost, he had heard. "And let's send out a big thank-you," he said, "to the generous taxpayers of this great land."

Talking to himself: an occupational hazard of the solitary stakeout. That and peeing in a soft drink can. Reece smiled, could feel a good routine coming on. Assuming he wanted to keep this narc-turned-comedian act going, which wasn't a sure thing.

Anyway: "The thing about these criminals?" Reece talked out loud again, practicing how he could tell the story on stage. "They're never on time. I mean, what's a schedule to drug addicts? I waited half the cold-ass day in my car for one named Jeter Pitts to show. Had to piss so bad I thought I'd pop. Only container in the car was a plastic cup, so I drained the old manly squirt-gun then and there, right into the cup. And wouldn't you know it, that's when Jeter Pitts shows up."

Right here, Reece thought, is where he would start to hear the first bit of laughter from the audience, get your giggles of anticipation. From the smart ones, anyway, who understand the comic possibilities of a cup of piss.

"So I take the cup and I place it on the dashboard. Then I step from the car and put the cuffs on him. No running, no resistance. Jeter Pitts just wants one thing, besides to get some more heroin. Jeter Pitts is just thirsty as hell."

Now, Reece thought, the laughter would start to build. He kept talking: "I got him cuffed in the backseat. He sees the cup, and says, 'What's that?' And I say, 'That, my friend, is Mountain Dew. You want a sip?' And Jeter says, 'Oh, *yeah*, man.'"

At this point, Reece could practically hear it already, the crowd is fucking rolling in the aisles. They're gasping for air when he tells them how heroin addicts can't smell worth a damn. And how Jeter Pitts looks at the cup and says, "Man, they is steam coming off that Mountain Dew." And how Reece comes back with, "You ain't never had *hot* Mountain Dew, Jeter? Hot Mountain Dew is the best kind."

They'll be fucking holding their sides in pain.

The only question with this bit was if he should use an actual glass of water when he imitated Jeter Pitts taking a sip. Because if he used actual water, he could do a Danny Thomas–grade spit-take, maybe get the people in the front row wet.

This, Reece told himself, was going to be one killer routine. This was—holy shit, there was action at the Driftwood. Time to go to work.

Reece raised the government binoculars. The door to Room 119 had opened, and after a few seconds a woman walked out. Reece tightened the focus on the glasses. And was knocked out by what he saw.

After days of searching, after half a dozen cold leads and rabbit trails, he finally had Angelique Joy. "Bitch in the sights," Reece said.

The decision he had to make now: follow her on foot or with the car. Better stay with the car, Reece thought. You try to hoof it, and she jumps into some wheels, you're screwed.

She crossed the Driftwood parking lot. Angelique wore a black T-shirt, tight jeans, and white deck shoes, and she moved like someone with all the time in the world. Reece started his car and inched forward just enough to keep her in sight.

At the front entrance to the Driftwood, she took a right, speeding up a little, headed for the restaurant next door, Mr. Chow's To-Go. With Reece talking out loud, "Chinese guy in bed with his wife, tells her, give me some sixtynine. Wife says, You want beef with broccoli *now*?"

Angelique went straight inside Mr. Chow's. Fucking place had plate-glass windows, but they were plastered with posters: KUNG PAO SPECIAL, $3.99. FRIED RICE WITH EGG ROLL, $4.99. Reece couldn't see a thing in there.

He gave her a couple of minutes, then a couple more. Finally Reece parked the car and went to the door of Mr. Chow's. It opened, and a customer came out, but not Angelique. Reece caught a glimpse of the inside before the door closed: a couple of tables, some plastic chairs, an order counter and a cash register, the kitchen working behind it. Two Chinese people inside, and no Angelique. He walked in.

"Where's the blondie?" he said to an old man behind the counter. With the old guy giving him a look that said unless Reece was ordering egg rolls, he wasn't interested. Reece turned to a young woman at the register. "The blonde chick," he said.

She turned and looked toward the back, all Reece needed. He went behind the counter, through the tiny kitchen and out the back door. The smell of wet garbage was in the air.

To the right was the back end of the Driftwood Motel, to the left a potholed parking lot. He heard the sound of a car starting. Headlights came on and swept over Mr. Chow's back wall when the car began to move. Reece ran, trying to catch the car as it pulled away.

The car dipped in and out of a concrete swale, then turned onto a side street. Reece stopped running; he was breathing hard, cramping up. The last thing he saw from the car: an arm extended from the window as Angelique Joy shot him the bird.

Reece watched the car go, then kicked at an empty bottle on the pavement. Some asshole would have to pay now, guess who.

He went back through Mr. Chow's, got his car, and drove the half block to the Driftwood. At Flippo's room, five knocks on the door, no answer.

"Open up, shit-attack." Reece slipped the lock and shoved the door open. Big entrance, but wasted on an empty room. Flippo was gone, and so were all his belongings.

Reece picked up a lamp and smashed it against the wall. Next he bolted for the Driftwood Motel office, flashed his badge at the clerk, and said, "Where's the fuckface from room 119?"

"Checked out," the clerk said, bored. "Not five minutes ago."

They had a pretty good laugh over Reece the schmuck running after them in the parking lot. A guy with legs that short, Jack said, should never try to chase a car.

Angelique smiled. "You and me, baby, we're a team."

Now they were in the lot of the Sea Lanes Bowling Alley, where Angelique had told Jack to go. "I'm gonna get out of the car, watch you drive off," she said. She kissed him and ran a finger along the top of his big nose. "Be a good boy and leave," she said as she opened the door. "But just for a little while."

She got out of the car and stood on the sidewalk, leaned in through the window, and said, "Remember. Sundown tomorrow."

"It's a date," he said.

Angelique watched him go, following his taillights until the car disappeared in traffic. In a few minutes, a red Camero rolled up and stopped. Angelique opened the passenger's side door and got in. Then she leaned across and kissed Lizette on the cheek.

"Well?"

"Well." Angelique took a big breath and let it out. "He's everything I remembered and more."

"What's that mean?"

"It means," she said, "that by this time tomorrow night, you and I should be having the party of our lives."

The best story I've ever done, I mean the *best*, and you didn't even see it?" Miranda tried to slam her refrigerator door shut but managed only a rubber-and-magnet smack and a light tinkling of glass bottles. "Are you blind?" she said. "It was just the top of the fucking front page."

"I was otherwise occupied," Jack said. Thinking, Let's see, there was the body in the landlocked submarine, followed by the body not in the landlocked submarine. Then Angelique dropping by to chew over old times. Then they had to make the quick exit from the Driftwood while Reece Pepper ran in circles.

After all that, Jack had driven to Miranda's and met her just as she came home from work. He was hoping for a couple of hours that might pass calmly; his head hurt and he was tired of surprises. Then he made the mistake of telling her he hadn't seen her story.

Now, still in the kitchen, she said, "Maybe the next time somebody tries to kill me you could at least notice. Do you even read the paper?"

"Of course I read the paper." Jack took two beers from the counter and followed Miranda toward the door. "I like that little mixed-up word puzzle on the comics page. What do they call that, Scramlets? Sometimes that thing can tear up an afternoon, you know it?"

"That story's gonna get me some notice, you watch."

"The intruder," Jack said, "who do you think it was?"

"He didn't leave his card. Which you would know if you'd bothered to read the story." Miranda made her way out the back door, letting go of it just as Jack came through, so that if he hadn't put his hands up it would have hit him in the face. "Now," she said, "if I can follow it with a killer piece on our man Wesley—"

"Something's about to happen on that."

Miranda stopped and turned. "Like what?"

Jack looked up; the clouds were clearing, the stars beginning to show. "I should know by tomorrow. I'll tell you then."

"You piece of crap." She put her hands on her hips. "You're trying to cut me out of this, aren't you?"

They pulled out chairs and sat at the patio table in the dark. Jack said, "Do you mistrust everybody? Or just me?"

"Everybody."

Jack nodded. "Yeah. Me, too."

"Hey, sweet talk won't work here. You never answered my question." Miranda fired up a cigarette, and Jack caught her face in the light from the match. She was looking at him as if her car had been stolen an hour before he arrived counting a wad from the chop shop.

"What is it," she said, "that you're not telling me?"

Jack sipped his beer, looked away, then came back to Miranda. She still had him in her sights. Finally he said, "You sure you want in on this?"

Miranda took another drag and gave him the answer with her stare.

Jack said, "I was going to give you a chance to walk away—"

"Forget it."

"—because I thought maybe the guy who tried to jump you the other night might have got you a little spooked."

"I looked spooked to you?"

Jack suddenly felt enormous pity for her ex, Allen the accountant. Guy was probably off in a quiet room somewhere, still shaking, scared as hell that he'd wake up in the morning, see her lying next to him, and realize the divorce was just a dream.

"No," Jack said, then gave a thin smile that she probably couldn't see in the dark. "You look ready for action."

She stubbed the cigarette butt in an ashtray. "About time you said the right thing."

"Got a few things I have to put together first."

"Name one."

"I need a boat."

"What kind of boat?"

"One that runs and doesn't leak."

"All right," she said, "what else?"

"Not quite sure yet."

Another match went to another cigarette. "Bad enough I got those no-clue morons at the paper telling me what to do," she said. "Now here comes another one."

"I'll tell you as soon as I can."

"So what you're telling me is I have to trust you on this."

"Trust is not such a bad thing," Jack said, "especially when there's no other choice."

She was quiet for a while. Jack could hear distant traffic, a car door slamming, a dog barking, air conditioners humming. He decided to change the subject, show his sensitive side. "Since you did get attacked and all"—he glanced around—"maybe you shouldn't stay here tonight. Know what I'm saying?"

"No."

"You got any friends you could stay with?"

"So the guy can follow me there and attack them, too?"

"How about a hotel?"

"Don't worry. He comes back again, I'll be ready for him. And no trailer-park blowtorch next time. Next time, bullets. That gun's got a permanent place under my pillow."

Jack sighed and shook his head. "Fine. If the second visit happens, I hope you live to write the story. For that one, I'll buy the paper."

Miranda coughed. "If it happens again it'll be a magazine piece."

"I gotta go find a new motel," Jack said. "I'll call you tomorrow."

"I need a swim," Miranda said. She stood and slipped off her jeans and pulled off her shirt. All Jack saw in the dark was her silhouette against a streetlight. He looked away anyway, trying to be polite for once.

"I need it bad," she said. Jack stood. Miranda eased down the pool's steps and into the blackness of the water. Saying, "God, this feels good." Then, to Jack, "Do me a favor on your way out. Turn the pool lights on."

"Have fun. Stay safe." Jack flipped a switch just outside the door, catching a glimpse of the watery turquoise light as he turned to go inside. He left to the sound of Miranda moving through the water.

He was walking through the kitchen, headed for the front door, when he heard her screams—not shrieks, but curses strung together, full of fear, like someone who had stepped into a nest of snakes.

Jack ran back outside. Miranda was out of the pool, standing at the edge and pointing down at the water. At the deep end, ten feet down, upright as if it were balancing on the drain, was the body of a man.

At first Jack thought B. T. Mack had been dumped back in his lap again. But a second look told him this was someone else.

The dead man's eyes were open, his mouth slack. He was fully dressed and hung in the water like an oversized fetus in a jar.

"I know the face," Jack said.

"Who is it? Who?" Miranda had pulled her clothes back on.

Jack leaned closer to the water. "Don't tell me. I've got it right on the tip of my tongue."

"Who?" she demanded

He studied the man's small eyes and his large lips. Jack looked away for a moment, recalling faces from the courtroom. Mugs on parade, his little trip down memory lane: child molesters, wife-beaters, car hot-wirers, and hot-check writers. He remembered a pig thief he had convicted and a pigeon-dropper who had walked. Jack ran a quick scan of every murderer he had put away, but none of them matched.

"You gonna come up with something one of these days?" Miranda said.

Jack turned back toward the water and surveyed the dead man's face one more time. That's when the I.D. came to him, as clear as if the guy had been wearing a name tag.

He stood and brushed the knees of his pants. "That man at the bottom of your pool?" he said to Miranda. "Say hello to Arthur Murry Murray. Or I guess good-bye would be more like it."

"TWO BODIES IN TWO days," Police Lieutenant Torres said. "That doesn't strike you as a little odd?"

"Odd? Sure." Jack rubbed his eyes. Another night with no sleep. "Since when do you arrest for odd?"

"You're not under arrest," Torres said.

"Hey," Jack said, "at least this body didn't disappear. So we're doing better. Don't suppose, by the way, you ever found the other one."

They were back in the same holding room, Jack and the lieutenant, who was looking tired himself. Tired of Jack, at least. He said, "And this was someone you knew."

"I sent him to prison once, maybe ten years back. Assault with intent, if memory serves, with the weapon of choice a brick. Or maybe a brake shoe, I'm not sure. The lowlifes all run together after a while. You get your machete killings mixed up with your meat–cleaver attacks."

"Seen him since?" Torres asked.

"Not till his watery gig last night."

The lieutenant shook his head but kept his eyes on Jack. "Something you're not telling me here."

Jack sniffed. "I'll admit, it looks strange. Tell you the truth, I wouldn't want to be in your shoes, trying to sort all this out. Though, come to think of it, I am."

"Am what?"

"Trying to sort all this out."

"And why would that be?"

"Like I said last time we met, just doing some work for a client."

Torres was about to say something else when one of the detectives rapped on the window that fronted the squad room. "Sit tight," he told Jack and walked out.

Jack stayed on the wooden bench, watching through the window as Torres talked to the detective. Both studied a sheet of paper the detective held. Then Torres went to the phone on the nearest desk and made a call. Ten minutes later, he was back in the holding room. He sat on the bench and told Jack, "Your lucky day."

"Another one?"

"The dead man's prints matched a latent we pulled off Miss Glass's back door after she had her encounter with the intruder."

"You see her story on that? Front page."

Torres massaged one temple. "So it seems he was back for an encore and just fell in the pool."

"Looked to me," Jack said, "like he'd been in the water for a while."

"Maybe the autopsy will turn up some trauma." The lieutenant stood. "Until then, accidental drowning is all we have. And the fact that you two met again after all these years? I guess we'll have to put that down to coincidence."

"You're stretching for that one, aren't you?"

Torres showed an unhappy grin. "You have a better theory?"

"Not yet," Jack said. "But it's early."

He walked out of the Galveston police station at six o'clock in the morning, the sun rising on a free man one more time. Miranda was standing next to her car, waiting for him.

"You doing okay?" he asked.

"Not bad considering."

"Want to grab some coffee?"

"Hop in," she said.

Jack pulled down the sun visor and checked the mirror. He saw a red-eyed, wild-haired dude who seemed in need of state hospital electroshock. That's the way you're supposed to look, he told himself, when the bodies start to pile up, and there's money and love on the line.

"By the way," Miranda said as she started the car, "I think I found you a boat."

The Brunson Bait Shop was a low, white cinder-block building on Offat's Bayou. Hand-lettered signs taped to the front window, in faded black marker on yellowed poster board, said, LIVE SHRIMPS FRESH CHICKEN NECKS and HEY DONT FORGET YOUR WORMS.

Miranda parked at the side of the crushed oyster-shell lot and led Jack to a dock behind the bait shop. Telling him, "I think this guy is in the mood for a favor."

At the dock Jack saw a fifteen-foot powerboat with a big Evinrude outboard. It looked to be about as old as he was. The boat was blue, with red cursive lettering painted on its side: HAPPY FAMILY.

"There she is," someone was shouting. Jack turned to see a huge guy—black, and mid-forties, at least 250 pounds—bearing down on Miranda. The man grabbed her and lifted her feet from the ground in a bear hug. Saying, "Bless you," and, "Praise God."

Jack watched them hug and laugh and waited for Miranda to introduce them and give him the quick fill: Kenny Brunson owned the bait shop. With his wife, he ran a foster home for ten teenage boys whose parents were dead or on drugs. They spent a lot of time teaching the kids about the water, but they badly needed a new boat.

"Which," Miranda said to Jack, "was another front-page story of mine I'm sure you missed."

"Man called yesterday morning," Brunson said, "and told us he was sending in a donation because of your story. Ask me how much."

"Tell me," Miranda said.

Brunson beamed. "Two thousand dollars, praise God."

"Get out."

Brunson turned to Jack. "I'm telling you this lady is special."

"Don't I know it," Jack said.

"I mean we're lucky to have her among us."

"Oh, I'm with you on that."

Miranda glanced around. "Where's the kids?"

"All in school," Brunson said. He and Miranda laughed about her visit; one of the boys had been desperate to shoot off some of the boat's safety flares.

"He was just dying to pull the trigger on that thing," Miranda said. "That kid had one itchy finger."

Brunson gave the name of each boy, then listed his food preferences and favorite TV programs. Good kids, Brunson said, who would never have a chance otherwise.

Miranda said Brunson was doing God's work.

Jack looked at his watch. Saying to Miranda, "I need to get going."

"You shoulda stayed around the other day," Brunson told Miranda. "Thunderstorm blew in, kept us outta the boat. So I sat the boys down and told them about the big 1900 hurricane. Shoulda seen their eyes when I gave them the story of the Catholic orphanage." To Jack, "You know that one?"

Jack shook his head. Saying, "You know, I really have to hit the road."

Brunson began to tell it anyway, deep voice and slow words. With the hurricane beginning to build, he said, the nuns running the orphanage had horrible visions of small boys and girls being washed away. So they said their prayers, then roped themselves to groups of children. Ten nuns would thus keep ninety orphans safe.

But when the storm had passed, after a wall of water had washed over Galveston, the beachfront orphanage was nothing but a pile of sticks. And dead children tied to dead nuns were found all over the island.

Miranda gave Jack an elbow. "All roped together with trouble on the way," she said. "Remind you of anyone?"

Jack was tired enough to drop in his tracks. But no time for sleep now. In a few minutes he was on the bridge over Galveston Bay, heading off the island.

For the first hour or two, the scenery wasn't much more than oil refineries and Houston sprawl. He stopped for breakfast around nine o'clock outside Port Arthur at some joint the health inspectors must have missed. The menu was illustrated with a smiling cartoon pig. Jack looked at it and saw the face of Arthur Murry Murray at the bottom of the pool.

"Just coffee," he told the waitress.

By eleven o'clock in the morning, Jack was just a few miles from Luster. But he got stuck behind a slow-moving log truck on the two-lane into town. That gave him, as he wound his way through the piney woods, some extra time to think. Which he really didn't want.

Extra time meant he could look that much closer at what he was doing, and what he was doing couldn't have withstood more than a quick glance.

This whole business, he recalled, had started out as a dimly understood noble gesture—helping a friend in need, making amends for an old wrong, all that. Then Angelique showed up.

He had done this before, with other women. Each time it felt as if he were being pulled into a dark shaft. The truth was, he liked the fall. He didn't always care where he ended up: divorce court, bankruptcy, singing along with loser drunks in blues bars. But he got a high-voltage charge out of the trip down.

Jack had never hunted big game or climbed mountains. He didn't do drugs and stayed away from the casinos. But he hunted women, climbed women, did women, bet on women. Something about being in the clutch of passion and appetites, and making a wreck of his life, gave him a thrill he couldn't live without. The sex wasn't bad either.

So now he was coming to Luster to seal the case, as much as he could, against Wesley. Seal the case so he could clear his conscience enough to run off with the guy's wife. Jack tried to tell himself that Wesley's guilt would cancel out his own bad action, as if there were some moral-code fine print somewhere that said wife-stealing was permissible when the husband commits a felony. If anybody else had worked that reasoning on him, Jack would have died laughing.

All right, it wasn't exactly a courageous crusade for justice and freedom anymore, this trip to Luster. It was no longer a case of Jack's ensuring that his aggrieved friend got a fair shake under the law, with Angelique as a bonus throw-in. Now he was more like a junkie stealing from Grandma.

At least no one was around to heap on the ridicule he deserved. He could imagine what Wesley might say to him: Who're you pretending to be with all this crap about justice, the Patrick Henry of pussy? What you've got, Wesley would have said, is a classic case of snatch poisoning.

She answered the phone with, "Miranda Glass."

"Honey," the man said, "I am really beginning to like the sound of your voice."

"This has to be Mr. Joy."

"Jackie says you're a cute one. I believe 'dish' is the word he used."

"I hear you're quite the spectacle yourself."

"Old Wesley tries. Though being a wanted man ain't doing my looks any favors. But, hey, how about when this is all over, once I get a chance to clean up a bit, you and me could have a drink together?"

"Well . . ." she said and froze. She thought she saw Ed Merritt coming her way.

"Don't have to say yes or no now. From what I heard on the radio this morning, hon, it's a miracle you're talking at all."

"I'm all right."

"Son of a bitch, whoever he was, deserved it for what he did to you. Deserved it for some other stuff, too, I'm willing to bet."

"Did you see my story about him?"

"You bet I did. Best damn writing this old boy has read in a long time."

Jesus Christ, Miranda thought, finally—someone who appreciates what she's trying to do. "Thank you."

"Hey, if old Wesley wasn't already in love with you for your voice, he'd fall for the way you write."

Miranda twisted the phone cord around her finger and leaned back in the chair. "I'm starting to like you, too," she said.

"One thing I was wondering, do the police know how it happened?"

"They're not quite sure yet. They still have to get the autopsy results."

"Old Wesley feels for you. All you're trying to do is relax, right? Just trying to get a little swimming in, and this piece of garbage has to turn up in the deep end."

With Miranda thinking, How did he know where the body was? She said, "At least I don't have to worry about him anymore."

"I like your attitude. You girls with spunk, old Wesley has a thing for that. That drink we talked about is sounding better and better."

"Any time."

"I got a feeling, hon, about you and me. I see something special down the road. Just maybe."

When Wesley had said good-bye, Miranda walked out of her office without telling anyone where she was going, and drove to the county courthouse. Ten minutes in the clerk's office, and she had the file she wanted: *State of Texas v. Arthur Murry Murray*.

Lieutenant Torres had told her about the case, a sexual assault complaint dismissed when the victim decided she wasn't talking after all.

Miranda was looking for material for her tale of the intruder part two. But then she saw the name of Arthur's lawyer, staring at her on the first page: Wesley Joy.

That changed everything. Miranda closed the file and walked to the pay phone in the hallway. It was time to wrap this story up.

NOT MUCH HAD CHANGED in Luster, it seemed to Jack. Downtown looked just as tired and shabby as it had on the previous trip. His first stop this time was the district attorney's office. D.A. Billy Fletcher was at his desk, wearing the same red bow tie he had on the last time Jack talked to him.

"Well, well," he said after Jack was waved in by the secretary. "I have to say I was surprised when you called for an appointment. Is Mr. Joy ready to turn himself in?"

"Not just yet."

"No?" Billy Fletcher raised an eyebrow. "Then why are you here?"

"Just checking up. Has Wesley been charged with murder? I'd like to see the particulars."

"Last time I looked, Mr. Joy had filed to represent himself. Are you Mr. Joy's legal counsel now?"

"I'll be submitting notice this week." Lies came out his mouth, Jack thought, as easily as snakes out of a hole.

The D.A. laced his long, thing fingers on the desk. He said, "There have been some developments in Mr. Joy's case."

"For example."

They sat looking at each other and listening to the clock tick. "All right," Billy Fletcher finally said, "let's try it this way." He pushed his chair away from the desk, stood, turned, and opened the top drawer of a file cabinet.

While the D.A.'s back was to him, Jack reached across the desk. He nabbed half a dozen business cards from a small silver rack.

"I can tell you," Billy Fletcher said as he turned around, "that we'd like to talk to Mr. Joy."

"That's supposed to get everyone excited?"

Billy Fletcher studied his file. "We might look at reducing some of the charges against him in return for his testimony."

A knuckleball. Jack squinted and said, "You telling me what? He's not a murder suspect?"

"I'm saying we'd like to talk to him." Billy Fletcher closed his file. "That's all."

"You haven't indicted him."

"No," Billy Fletcher said.

Jack ran his fingers through his hair. Thinking that every time he had this case in his sights, it moved. He said, "Why not? I mean, you've got him in the goddamn dead guys' car. What are you waiting on?"

Billy Fletcher cleared his throat and blinked a few times. "You're his . . . *defense* counsel?"

Jack felt as if the floor were tilted and his chair was on rollers. "Reduce charges—what are you talking about? In exchange for what?"

The D.A. waited. Then, "When you're the attorney of record, we can talk in more detail."

Jack waved a hand. "Soon as my secretary can type it up."

Billy Fletcher nodded, then put on a stern face. Jack had seen it a hundred times, on everyone from judges to shrinks. "My advice to you and your friend? Get him in here," the D.A. said. "Time is not on Mr. Joy's side."

"Call me crazy," Jack said, "but I feel a dire warning coming on."

"Those two dead men were high-stakes drug dealers. This much absolutely no one disputes. The record speaks for itself."

Jack waited.

"Where are the drugs now?" Billy Fletcher said. "Where is the money now?"

Jack waited some more.

"Someone got killed for them once." Billy Fletcher segued from stern to smug. "I'd say there's a reasonable chance it could happen again."

The motel was on the east end of Luster, and it looked like a thousand other dumps you found beside the highways in Texas. The sign out front had Carefree in cursive white neon, and below that the red letters on the marquee said AMERICAN OWNED. Proving once again, it seemed to Jack, that when it came to run-down, tank-town tourist courts, U.S.A. was number one.

If there had been an eyewitness, this would be the likely place to find him. That was Jack's best guess, anyway. Maybe he would find Billy Fletcher's developments, whatever they were. Maybe he would stumble onto something the small-town cops had overlooked.

Jack parked, went to the motel office, and found a gray fat woman with a seen-it-all expression behind the front desk. A rectangular plastic tag pinned to her blouse said she was Velma the manager. Sweat and powder made a thin cake in the soft folds of her neck. Velma was doing the books and watching an aerobic workout show.

Jack smiled and placed one of Billy Fletcher's business cards on the glass atop the counter. "That's right," he said. "Back for just a few more questions."

She looked away from the TV long enough to read the card and glance at Jack's face. Then back to the workout with, "Herman's in the shed."

"Of course he is," Jack said. "He wouldn't be Herman if he wasn't. Now which shed would that be?"

"Same one he was in last time you people come and talked to him."

"Like I said. Just a few more questions."

She rotated her head his way and fixed him with tiny eyes that counted every dime. "Last time," she said, "you people kept Herman talking for one solid hour. That's one hour's work I didn't get out of him."

"No problem. See the address on that card?" Jack tapped it with his finger. "Send the tab to Mr. Billy Fletcher. He'll pay for Herman's time himself."

She picked the card up, from garbage to cash in an instant, and set it on the open account book. "Might have been two hours they was talking," she said.

"Make it four," Jack said and left the office. He wandered the grounds a few minutes before finding the shed behind the motel.

It was a one-car garage sagging to the left, with walls of peeling clapboard and a floor of old roofing shingles laid on dirt. A mattress and a box spring leaned against the wall, and yard tools hung from nails. A man in a greasy T-shirt stood at a workbench, oily fingers in the scattered parts of a lawn mower engine.

"What do you say, Herman?" Jack called before the man saw him. "You doing all right today?"

The man turned, stepped into the sun, and spit some brown juice into the weeds. After a while he said, "This about that car payment?"

"Wouldn't do that to you," Jack said.

"I told Elmer I'd bring it by Monday."

"Not busting nobody's chops today," Jack said. "Not even for Elmer."

Herman stood there with a face that said every day brought its own special share of shitty news, and today's hadn't been delivered yet. He had a half-week's worth of white stubble, and faded tattoos crawled up skinny arms. On his forehead was a growth that looked like a grape caught beneath the skin.

Jack could tell in an instant that Herman had been prime bad-ass in his day, but now he was all clogged lines and fouled plugs.

"Here you go," Jack said as he tried to hand him one of Billy Fletcher's cards. When Herman didn't take it, Jack placed it on the workbench and asked, "Got a minute to talk?"

"About what?"

"Those two boys that got shot up here a while back."

"I done told everything I know."

"I know that. But the boss sent me out here just to make sure we didn't forget anything."

"I done told everything."

Jack rubbed the back of his neck. The sun was a bastard out here. "That Miss Velma in the office"—he motioned with his head—"she ever give you a dinner break?"

More brown juice went to the ground. "Half an hour."

Jack took his car keys from his pocket and gave them a jingle. "How about this: Let's grab us a six-pack from the mini-mart and call it lunch?"

———

Reece Pepper was counting up his problems, starting with the dead cop in the deep-freeze and proceeding to the snitch who had disappeared. He had lost track of Angelique, Wesley, and Flippo, making him an absolute loser in the tailing game. If he was a religious man, he would have prayed: Dear Lord in Heaven, help me find these fucking motherfuckers.

The phone rang. Reece answered and found salvation on the line. He knew that as soon as the woman said, "This is Miranda Glass. I have something to tell you."

In the parking lot of the Gas-N-Git, they sat in Jack's car with the air conditioner going. Herman ate a microwaved burrito and drank a can of Pearl, which loosened him up right away. He said to Jack, "You the first of them boys from the D.A.'s office that ain't a spray can full of aerosol shit."

"If you can't buy a man a beer now and then," Jack said, "then what's the use of working for Billy Fletcher?"

Herman nodded and kept after the burrito. The beer was between his legs. "First ones was all over me because I didn't say what I seen right away."

"No need to rush these things. How long did you wait?"

"Few weeks, maybe, I don't know."

"Why that long?"

"Why you asking me that?" Herman looked sideways. "Them boys you work with didn't tell you anything?"

"I'm just checking," Jack said, "to see if they got it right."

"Well"— he paused for a swallow —"did they tell you it was because of that lying asshole deputy B. T. Mack?"

"Sure. But give it to me again."

"All goes back to that time he arrested my brother Vernon." Herman sighed. "All right, Vernon knows he shouldn't of exposed hisself in front of that schoolteacher."

"Showing remorse. That's a good sign."

"He'd been drinking a little, had to take a piss, and forgot to put Rover back in his pants. That's all. Vernon turns around and there the teacher lady is. I mean, she come out of nowhere, lightning fast. Her and her grandma."

"Could happen to anyone," Jack said.

"Hey, don't you ever forget to put something back where you found it?"

"You kidding? Every day."

"B. T. Mack made the arrest. Next thing we know, Vernon's down at the jail with a broke leg. B. T. said he stepped on him by accident. Now tell me why everbody believes B. T. and not Vernon."

Jack remembered B. T.'s face in the belly of the submarine: blue-white in the middle of the flashlight beam, eyes bugged out and bloodshot, rope around his neck. That one he'd probably see in his dreams for a while.

Vernon said, "Then, that night everything busted loose at the motel, B. T. Mack's hustling around like the big man, asking questions. What I'm supposed to do, be nice to him? And forget all about Vernon?"

"So you clammed up."

"After a while, I decided to talk to the D.A."

"Civic duty?"

"Well, that and they said they was gonna revoke my parole if I didn't."

Herman was one of those talkers, it seemed to Jack, that you had to keep tethered. He said, "You mind summing it up for me? What you saw that night."

"I seen 'em go down, and I seen who did it."

Jack sat up straight. "You actually saw the shooter fire the gun."

"Oh, yeah."

"Clear enough to make an I.D. in court?"

"Even when my mind gets a little fuzzy, my eyes is sharp."

Here it was, what he had come for. "Let's get the description down first, then we'll move to the action," Jack said, "When you saw the shooter, did he still have his long hair?"

"Huh?"

"The shooter. He has short hair now, but when you saw him it was probably long and gray."

Herman sipped his Pearl, then said, "Run that one by me again."

Jack opened his own can of beer. Thinking that Herman might have sniffed too many gas fumes back there in the shed. "All right, let's try this. Did the shooter have a patch over his eyes?" He got a blank gaze from Herman. "Was he, you know, doing the Long John Silver thing?"

Herman nodded. "They got one in Beaumont."

It was Jack's turn for an empty stare.

"Long John Silver's," Herman said. "I used to date this gal loved fish food. Tell you what, though, I go for beef myself. You gonna eat that other burrito?"

"All yours." Jack blew some air. "Call it a hunch, Herman, but I got a feeling that we're not tuned to the same channel."

Herman rested the second burrito on his thigh and pulled another can of Pearl from its plastic ring. "How about I just tell it to you from the jump."

"Whenever you're ready."

Herman wiped his mouth with the back of his wrist. "Make a long story short, my old lady was all over my ass that night. Would not get off. So I said, screw this, I'll go sleep in the shed."

"Every man needs a refuge."

"Don't I know it. Now, right when I'm settling in for the evening, I hear commotion from unit five. I mean loud. People having a fight or one hell of a bad party. I stroll over, see if I can make out what the problem is."

"You're curious."

"No, I wanted them people to shut up so I could sleep."

"You went to their door?" Jack said, trying to speed it up.

"Nuh-uh. I'm back of the motel, remember, and who the hell wants to walk all the way around?"

Jack waved a hand, giving up.

"I go up to the bathroom window instead," Herman said. "It's open about two foot, so I could see into the whole unit. Tell you what, that's where the action was."

"Action," Jack said. "Now we're getting somewhere."

Herman took a bite of burrito but kept talking. "Big old dude, he's begging, 'Don't kill me.' Well, it don't work. 'Cause it's *bang* and he falls on the bed."

"Shot," Jack said.

"What else you think bang means?"

"Never mind," Jack said. "What happened next?"

"Next thing, another dude comes into the picture. This one's skinny, and he's running like hell for the bathroom. Son of a bitch is coming right at me. I back up, but he keeps coming and coming, till he's trying to climb right through the window. That's when I heard two more shots. The boy went limp in a hurry."

"He's dead," Jack said.

"Or doing a damn good impression."

"Let's get this straight." Jack waited for Herman to turn his way. "The first one that got it—you saw who shot him, right?"

"I didn't say that."

"Hold on. Then you *didn't* see who shot him?"

"I didn't say that, neither."

With Jack thinking, Jesus Christ, this guy put the pecker in peckerwood. He cleared his throat and said, "You're right, you didn't say one way or the other. Maybe you'd like to say it now?"

Herman scratched his belly. "Matter of fact, I saw the shooter get the big one twice."

"Good. Now. Here's the question. What did he look like?"

"Who?"

Jack rubbed his face and took a breath. Then said slowly, "The shooter. What did he look like?"

"*He* didn't look like nothing."

Jack stared. Herman said, "Know why?"

"Don't want to even guess."

Herman smiled, showing his brown teeth. He seemed proud of himself. "'Cause that *he* you keep talking about? That was a *she*."

"What? A woman fired the gun?"

"Yep. Nailed that boy solid, too."

"You sure it wasn't a man with long hair?"

"With titties?"

Jack felt as if he were watching someone cart his insides away in a truck. The thing to do now, he told himself, was tell Herman thanks, put him out of the car with the rest of the six-pack, and drive away. Forget he ever met the man.

Herman said, "She was pretty good-looking for a slut with a gun. Personally, I like mine unarmed."

With Jack thinking, Can't be. And, Don't do it. But he did. He reached into the backseat, into his briefcase, and came back with the picture he had of Angelique and her dark-haired friend: the two of them, standing on the deck of the sailboat.

He said, "Take a look, Herman."

Herman peered at the photo for a few seconds, then laughed. "Shit, you knowed it was her the whole time. You was just stringing me along."

Jack kept the picture in front of Herman. "Which one?" he said.

"Oh, we still playing that game, huh? All right." He put a dirty fingernail on Angelique's face. "That's your pistol-packin' mama." He smiled. "Remember that song?"

Jack had the sensation of floating up above the car, looking down on himself. Staring, he thought, at some-one who, if the vote were held today, would be a shoo-in for sucker of the year. And eligible by now for the life-time achievement award.

Herman brought Jack back into the car with a belch.

"Hey," Herman said, "your boys tell you what she said before she shot the fat one? Remember?"

All Jack could do was shake his head.

"Oh, man," Herman said, "she was yelling at him, 'Where's the fucking money?'" He barked a little laugh. "Tell you the truth, she didn't give him much of a chance to answer. The girl with the gun? I don't think being patient was what she done best."

HE HAD GALVESTON ALMOST in sight by mid-afternoon and could remember almost nothing of the previous three hours. The drive from Luster had passed as if he were in a trance, with the midday light unchanging, the highway straight and flat, and Jack deep inside his head. He had spent the time replaying the voices of Wesley and Angelique and everyone else from the last four days, taking what he remembered and listening to every pause, blurt, and dip, as if their words were the tumblers of a safe he was trying to crack.

About Wesley—Herman said he could see the whole motel room and there wasn't a one-eyed guy in sight. So Wesley went back into the not-guilty column. Jack had moved him back and forth enough times now that there were ruts. Not to mention shame.

But how much not guilty? Wesley had been in the dead men's car in Luster, and that still hadn't been explained.

Now, Angelique. Maybe Herman had been wrong about her. A man who guzzled beer and slept in a shed might not be the best source of information. Hey, the dude had a goiter.

Not to mention that every trial lawyer knew that an eye-balled I.D. of a suspect was unreliable. Witnesses thought they saw people they really didn't see. All the time they did this. A lot of your feebs couldn't tell the difference between *might be* and *definitely is*. But they got on the stand anyway and decided close enough was good enough.

Maybe he should have questioned Herman more closely, should have shaken him out of his certainty. But there was no reason for that. The Luster D.A. would believe what he wanted to believe. Jack would bet everything he owned, even if there wasn't a tax lien against it, that they wanted to arrest Angelique now.

But if Angelique was stone guilty, it made no sense for her to be hanging around. She should have set sail a long time ago—except for the drug money, which she believed Wesley had. How did he get it? How did she know?

And what difference did it make? None. All Jack could hope to do now was salvage the wreckage.

He dialed the number Wesley had given him. The woman who answered said it was the Tweety Motel and gave him Wesley's room. Wesley answered on the second ring.

"I've found her," Jack said.

"God bless you, my boy."

"I'll be there in an hour."

"I'll be waiting," Wesley said.

"Good," Jack said. "Have the two hundred thousand waiting with you."

"The hell you talking about?"

"I know you have it," Jack said. He hung up before Wesley could respond.

Jack drove the long bridge over the bay. There was a light chop on the water, and he could see refineries in the distance, with the sun still too high to turn the scene from industrial to exotic.

Just as his car touched Galveston Island, his phone began to ring. For a moment he was so caught in his own thoughts that he didn't recognize the sound. It registered as an irritation, like a fly buzzing around his head.

On the fourth or fifth ring he climbed out of his brain muck far enough to pull off the road and answer. Thinking it would be Wesley. "Yeah?"

"Mr. Flippo?" A man's voice.

"Yeah?"

"Roland Barnes with the Justice Department. Calling in regard to your query."

Jack didn't remember any Roland Barnes. And something about a query? His short-term memory was like a house somebody moved out of last week—nothing left now but dust balls, a bag of garbage, and the rats in the attic.

Jack had gone long enough without sleep that he was starting to feel as if he were adrift on another world. He had never noticed before how strange palm trees looked, like green sparklers—maybe, he wasn't sure, he lost his train of thought. For a second there he couldn't be certain that he was driving on the right side of the road. And the signs on the convenience stores and gas stations seemed to be in a tongue he only dimly recalled.

It suddenly hit him that maybe ten seconds had passed with Roland Barnes still on the line, waiting. Jack managed, "Roland, my man. What's shaking?"

"You called"— Barnes paused, then cleared his throat — "our Houston office earlier this week."

With Jack thinking, I did? He said, "You bet."

"Asking about Agent Reece Pepper."

It came back to him now—his call, his question, and the official D.E.A. go-screw-yourself response. "That's right," Jack said.

"Your name and number were passed to me." Barnes had one of those clipped ways of talking that made Jack think of process servers in unmarked Plymouths. He pictured a guy with a salt-and-pepper flat-top above a pin-striped suit from the Sears catalog. Barnes said, "Do you have some information on Agent Pepper?"

"Information on Agent Pepper," Jack echoed. He almost added, That's what I called *you* to get. But he found the sense to say, "I might be willing to trade my stuff for yours."

Barnes didn't answer for a moment. With Jack thinking that one day they're treating him like an unemployed brother-in-law who wants to borrow money for the dog track. And the next day they're calling him, asking for help. Which meant he had some aces somewhere he didn't know about.

Finally Barnes said, "All right. We'll have an exchange."

"You first."

"Agent Reece Pepper," Barnes said, "was until a few years ago a D.E.A. operative serving in Mexico."

Barnes stopped talking. Jack said, "My turn? Now he seems to be hanging around Galveston. And here's your bonus nugget. He thinks he's funny."

"Where in Galveston?"

"Here and there."

"Where is he staying?"

"Not with me. That's all I know."

"Has he shown you a badge?"

"This your idea of trading information? What else you do for the government, man, negotiate Indian treaties?"

"I need to know," Barnes said, "if he has shown you a badge."

Jack thought back to the first meeting at Miranda's house. "He flashed it between funny stories."

"Did he show you an I.D. with Reece Pepper's name on it?"

"Why?"

Barnes cleared his throat again. "Are you free this after-noon?"

The man had moved from anxious to desperate, Jack thought. He said, "Free for what?"

"We'd like to send an agent down from Houston—"

"Forget it."

"—to visit with you. About Agent Reece Pepper."

"Not until I know why." Silence on the other end. "I'm hanging up now," Jack said.

"Don't do that," Barnes said.

"I will unless you start talking and don't stop till the story's done."

"Let us have someone—"

That was all Jack heard. He took the phone from his ear and pressed the disconnect button. Fifteen seconds later it was ringing again. Jack answered with, "Are you ready to spill, Roland?"

"Someone from our Houston office can be there—"

Jack hung up again. He put the phone on the seat next to him and waited. A minute passed, then two. He was wondering if he had overplayed his hand. Finally the ringing came once more.

"Absolute last chance," Jack said when he answered. "Next time I call-forward you to dial-a-prayer."

"Agent Reece Pepper," Barnes said, "worked under-cover in the Mexican state of Chihuahua."

"Until?"

"Two years ago. Which point he disappeared."

"I'm still with you," Jack said.

"Nineteen months after that," Roland Barnes said, "workers laying gas pipe outside Matamoros found a body buried in a field."

"Oh, boy." Jack could fill it in from there. "I.D.'d with?"

"Dental records."

Jack felt woozy. "So the comedian with the dead agent's badge—who's that?"

"We have a name."

"What name?" Jack said.

"We can't release that."

"You want my help or not?" Even as he asked the question, Jack knew he wouldn't have to wait for Roland Barnes, who was jawing on and on about confidentiality and how they didn't want to tip the suspect, and the only reason he would trust Jack with this info was his status as a former prosecutor.

Jack wasn't sure how, didn't know why or from where, but while Roland was talking, it came to him: the answer, like a bird winging in and settling on a perch outside his window.

He reached into his briefcase and found the bond papers he had taken from Angelique's purse, unfolding them as Barnes built up the disclosure.

"Only because you're an officer of the court," Barnes said, "am I going to give you the name of the suspect."

Jack held the bond paper and read the name typed in after "defendant." He moved his lips as Barnes finally said the words, too: Royal Curley.

"All right," Jack managed to say. Seeing himself back in one of those shafts again, still falling. He said, "Okay, this Royal Curley's the one with the badge. But does that mean he's the one who killed your agent?"

"We don't know yet." Barnes cleared his throat again. "My question to you is, where can we find him?"

Jack was like a guy hit so many times now that his eyes had swollen shut.

"His part of town, places he might go to," Barnes said. "Anything like that. How about associates?"

"You might try a place," Jack said, "called Sportin' Life Tavern. Or go to the Laff Factory in Houston."

"That supposed to be some kind of joke?" Barnes said.

Jack was wondering if he should tell Barnes to ask for Malcolm Ex-Husband.

The Sportin' Life, a few blocks from downtown: Miranda lit a Winston and blew smoke toward the low ceiling. "God, I feel so stupid."

"Hon, if it was a sin being stupid," Reece Pepper said, "we'd need a hundred times the churches we got now. My opinion? That's why stupid's not in the top ten commandments. It'd just be too much to handle."

"I guess."

"Instead we got covet thy neighbor's ass. Now, that one's not gonna draw the crowds, unless God was talking thy neighbor's *piece* of ass. Different story."

Miranda closed her eyes and took a drag. "Anyway. First time, I thought it was just a random perv attack, you know?"

"Don't have to be a member of professional law enforcement"—Reece tapped his chest twice—"to know that."

Miranda stopped and turned. "To know what?"

Reece went palms up. "What you just said, darlin'."

Miranda blinked a few times. "I mean, I write about this stuff all the time for the paper, twisted-dick rapists breaking into houses."

"Sure you do."

"So I thought this was one of those."

"Sure you did."

"My number coming up."

"Can say that again."

"He just happened to pick somebody who knew how to fight back."

"You showed the mother."

"Right. But then he comes back a second time," she said. "Same guy—"

"What? Wait a minute." Reece dropped his grin and raised his hand. "Slow down, now."

"Only this time I find him in my pool. In my pool and way dead."

"The same guy—*drownded*?" Reece looked as if all the air had leaked from him. He shook his head and muttered, "Shit, how'd the bastards find out?"

"What else when you're stiff in the water?" Miranda tapped the table twice. "That was bad enough, but here's what creeped me out extra. You ready? Flippo knew the dead guy. I.D.'d him on the spot, somebody named Arthur Murry."

"He did?" Reece leaned forward, head in hands. "Christ, nobody told me nothing about this."

"So I have a hunch, right? This morning I check some court records." Miranda mashed her cigarette into the ashtray. "Arthur Murry's lawyer? Guess who. The one and only Wesley Joy, that's who. . . . You all right?"

"I need another." Reece turned toward the bar and raised a finger. Then back to Miranda after a big sigh: "Well, now. Ain't the world full of surprises."

She nodded. "You got that right. I mean, all this time I'm working with these guys—"

"Big mistake."

"—and I'm going along with their plan."

"Which is?"

"Then this happens, and I see right away they're not coming clean with me. Some way, somehow, they're using me."

"Dirty as dirty fuckers can be."

"That's why I called you."

Reece reached across the table and patted her arm. "Don't worry about a damn thing, hon. Of all the places to come to, you picked the right one."

He knocked at the last room at the Tweety. Saying, "It's me."

Wesley opened the door. He was dressed in a black T-shirt and black jeans. "Jackie," he said. "You're a sight for a sore eye."

Jack stepped into the room, and Wesley closed the door. The only light came from the TV. "You have the money?"

Wesley pointed to a blue nylon overnight bag. "Right here, much as it pains me to say it."

After a moment, Jack said, "I'm sorry, man."

"What for?"

"For what I did to you."

Wesley backhanded the air. "You talking about putting the pork to Angelique?"

"That and some other things."

"Forget it."

"I'll make it up to you," Jack said. "Starting tonight."

THE BRUNSON BAIT SHOP was closed. Jack parked on the side, next to the big silver propane tank, and said, "Let's go for a boat ride."

He found the key to the *Happy Family* on a nail by the back door, right where Kenny Brunson had promised. At the dock, he and Wesley pulled a faded green canvas cover from the boat. "How old's this thing?" Wesley said. "I don't know I'd try to sail a boat this beat up across the bathtub."

"She's in fine shape." Jack primed the engine and turned the key. The motor caught, coughed a few times, and died. Blue smoke washed over them.

"Don't worry," Jack said, "it always does that."

"Gonna be dark soon." Wesley waved to clear the air and looked toward the water. "How far we going?"

Jack gave the motor another crank. There was more blue smoke, but no stall this time. He smiled at Wesley. "Right up to the edge," he answered.

Wesley nodded. "Shouldn't take long to get there. It's getting back that's usually the problem."

Angelique dropped anchor on La Ventana in a wide cove on the north side of Pelican Island, the spot she had drawn on the map for Jack. She asked Lizette, "You got those margaritas ready yet?"

"Working on them," Lizette called from the galley.

Angelique gazed across the water. The air was dead calm, the light in a slow fade. Half a mile away, the Bolivar Ferry chugged by on its way to the Galveston dock.

"Nice sunset," Lizette said. She handed Angelique a glass.

"Not bad for here." Angelique was thinking of a boy she had known at Texas Christian. Dumb but good-looking, like a lot of them at T.C.U. From a rich family in San Antonio, pledged Kappa Alpha, liked to shoplift convenience stores as a hobby. For spring break he had taken her to Puerto Vallarta, where they had watched sunsets on cocaine and mescal.

"They're better farther south," Angelique said. "Like everything else, you get what you pay for."

The wake of the ferry, what was left of it, finally reached the sailboat. Angelique felt the deck rise and drop gently under her feet.

"So," Lizette said. "Is tonight the night?"

"Well . . ." Angelique sipped, then smiled. "Jack told me he'd deliver."

"You're amazing," Lizette said.

Angelique smiled. "That's what Jack seems to think."

Reece Pepper turned left at Stewart Beach and drove north on Second Street. Saying, "Can't wait till I grab that one-eyed asshole."

Miranda, on the seat beside him, turned. "I'm surprised you want to handle this all by yourself."

"What I'm supposed to do?" Reece said. "Go hire some temps to help out? Call Kelly Girls and ask can they send over some gals to assist with a government bust?"

"I just thought you'd have the whole D.E.A. team out on this, that's all."

"And share the glory? No chance. Only room for one in this spotlight."

"Take a left here," Miranda said.

They were on a curving residential side street now. After a couple of blocks it dead-ended at the waterfront: a weedy county park with an old wooden dock and a boat ramp.

"Pull up on the grass," Miranda said. "Get as close to the dock as you can. That's where he told me they'd bring the boat to."

The park was empty except for them. To the right, a few hundred yards away, was the terminal for the Bolivar Ferry. One had just docked, and cars streamed off it, a few with headlights switched on in the near dusk. The cautious ones, Miranda thought, the people that lit them up a half-hour before the sun went down, just as the driver's manual said to do. Allen her ex had been that way.

If they looked straight ahead, Miranda and Reece had a clear view of the channel that passed between Galveston and Pelican Island. The water, half a mile wide, was turning from lead to gold as the sun sank.

"I'd guess within fifteen minutes," Miranda said with a glance at her watch.

Reece opened his door. "I'm gonna hop in the backseat, so they don't see me right away."

"While we're waiting," Miranda said after Reece had settled into the back, "I have a few questions for you."

"As long as one of them is, 'Reece, how come you so damn sexy?'"

Miranda looked into the rearview mirror. "Say Joy really did kill those two druggies—all right, fine. Then what's he been after in Galveston? I mean, he managed to skip jail, so why's he been hanging around here?"

Reece stared at the back of her head. Christ, this chick was even dumber than he thought. He started to say, Make an "S" on your reporter's pad, honey, and draw two lines through it. That'll be your answer.

Instead Reece said, "Gotta tell you something, this is the strangest case I've ever seen, bar none, all my years in law enforcement." Reece peered over the seat to see her writing in her notebook. "You getting all this?" he said. Oh, man, she was eating it up.

"Now one thing I need to mention." Reece sniffed. "Going back to your original question: The day Reece Pepper needs help making an arrest is the day Reece Pepper turns in his badge. You need me to repeat that? By the way, is your story gonna mention my rugged handsomeness?"

The *Happy Family* passed out of Offat's Bayou and into the open water of Galveston Bay. "Smooth sailing tonight," Wesley said.

Jack nodded. "Let's hope."

They rounded the point and headed east under the bay bridge, Jack steering. He said, "Here's one for you. You think it's ever too late to change your life? I don't mean a little bit. Talking all the way."

"That's why I came to Galveston, Jackie. Was gonna start over, put everything together for once. Believe it or not, I think I still can, even with the way everything's stacked against me right now. Gotta think every day's a new one."

Jack waited a moment. Ahead was another, smaller bridge, then the channel between Pelican Island and Galveston. It was almost time.

He said, "Wesley, you don't need Angelique anymore."

I think I see them." Miranda had Reece's binoculars pointed toward the water. "Hold on. . . . Yeah, that's the boat."

"Goody." Reece bent over and began to untie his shoe, glad that he was wearing ankle-highs laced with strong nylon cord. "Keep watching that boat," he told her. "Don't take your eyes off it."

He could use his gun on her, a little shot to the back of the skull, she'd never know what hit her. But, man, the mess it would leave in the car. Reece had made that mistake once, years ago. Ruined the upholstery of a 1988 Ford pickup. Luckily, it was the dead guy's truck, not his.

Miranda kept her gaze on the water. "Now the plan," she said, "is for Flippo to pull the boat to the dock. Joy'll get out, and Flippo will go on."

"Yeah? Well, the plan just changed." Reece pulled the lace from his shoe. "Nobody's going nowhere without the one and only me."

"All right, that's them, definitely," Miranda said. "They should be turning toward the dock right about now."

Reece, still bent over, wrapped the ends of the lace over his fists, four times around each hand.

"This way now," Miranda said. She still had the binoculars up. "Boys, the dock is over here. Come on, now. Don't go weird on me. Do not do this."

Reece tightened the lace and raised his hands, with his fists eighteen inches apart. He needed Miranda to lower the binoculars so he could go over her head in one quick motion, pull it tight against her throat, and wait for her to stop kicking.

"They're going too far," Miranda said. "Jesus Christ, what is this?" She threw the binoculars onto the seat. "They're not stopping!"

Reece lowered his hands. "Huh? What happened?"

"That lying fucker—" Miranda pushed the car door open. By the time Reece grabbed his gun, she was on the ground and running toward the ferry dock.

He was out of the car, right behind her, when his unlaced shoe came off. Reece had his gun in his hand, and she was only twenty feet away. He could have dropped her right there, no problem.

But there were people in cars rolling onto the ferry; they might see everything. Besides, he thought, no need to kill her now. She might come in handy later, you never knew.

He congratulated himself on his patience. That kill-before-thinking impulse was a bad habit he had worked all his adult life to overcome.

Reece went to one knee and did a quick lace-up. Then he was up and running after her.

What do you mean," Wesley said, "not need Angelique."

Jack stayed to the left of the channel, away from the dock that used to be important, boat at medium speed. "All this time you thought she could be your alibi."

"My only hope, Jackie. I mean, I'm like a sick dog, and she's the only sick-dog doctor in town."

"Not anymore."

"What's that mean?"

"They found a witness who saw the whole thing."

"Don't toy with me now, Jackie."

"You're clear."

"Knock me over." Wesley put his hands to his head. "Clear?"

"Maybe not on the jail escape. The heroin in the car, I don't know. But they don't have you for murder anymore."

Wesley's chest was rising and falling with big breaths. "A witness . . . A good one?"

"Motel handyman. I talked to him. He saw the killing, but he never saw you."

Wesley reached and pulled Jack into a hug. "Goddamn it, I knew you'd come through, Jackie. From the first, when you visited my jail cell. I knew you'd do it for old Wesley."

"There's more," Jack said.

Wesley released the hug. "We're gonna have some kind of blowout party, my friend. Boiled shrimp, Cuban cigars, and stippers from Houston. I mean class all the way."

"One more thing. She's the one."

"Who is?"

Jack watched his face. He said, "Angelique."

"Angelique's the one what?"

"The one who did the murders."

Wesley sagged against a seat. "Can't be."

"The witness makes her solid."

"There's just no way. I can't believe that."

"Me neither." Jack sighed and shook his head. "But the witness says it, and the D.A. believes it."

"Oh Lord." Wesley leaned against the side of the boat. After a while, "Angelique know about this?"

"Not yet."

"What she did?" Wesley said. "Probably all my fault somehow. I knew she'd took up with a bad crowd, got in with the serious partyers, and I didn't do a thing to stop it."

Jack looked straight ahead, giving Wesley time to absorb all the news, giving himself a chance to count the ways he had once more driven his life into a wall.

"It's a hard-won lesson, Jackie." Wesley rubbed his forehead like a man with migraines. "You just never know somebody, I don't care how close you are to them. I mean you can know every freckle, every hair, what they say in their sleep. But you can't say what they're capable of."

Miranda had run through two backyards and scrambled over a couple of chain-link fences. Now she loped across a parking lot as the last of the cars pulled onto the ferry. She yelled "Wait!" and waved her arms. No one seemed to notice.

She looked over her shoulder to see Reece Pepper maybe fifty feet back. Hot-shit undercover cop? He was just another fat slob now, sucking wind after a quick sprint.

The attendant was closing the low gate on the ferry. She tried shouting again and got nothing. There were a couple of blasts from the captain's horn as the ferry started to pull away, the diesel engine growling, the water churning at the stern. Miranda never broke stride.

At the edge of the dock she came down on her left foot, then sprang up and out, over the water.

In that moment she flashed on a memory, in and out of her mind like an electrical charge: She's seventeen, at the high school track and field county championships, Huntsville, Texas, under the lights on a warm spring night. Miranda's doing the broad jump, her third try, coming down the runway at full speed, hitting the launch stripe, and soaring.

She has that feeling that every jumper lives for, that slice of an instant when it seems as if you'll never come down.

Then she's into the sand pit. She rises to cheers. Miranda pumps her fist, and does a little dance. Telling herself, might be, could be, feels like a record jump. The best she's ever made, by far.

The celebration lasts five seconds or so, until she sees the face of the judge. He's shaking his head; Miranda's toes had been over the line.

But now: Her right foot landed on the lip of the ferry deck. Her left slipped. She had both hands on the railing. She pulled herself over and tumbled onto the deck.

Miranda rose and brushed herself off. She went to the rail, looking down at the water and back at the dock. Saying out loud, "Shit, I made it easy."

Then thought, Yeah, and now what?

Reece Pepper couldn't believe it; the bitch had actually jumped. And made it. And sailed away. While he was left here in fuck-you city, with nothing to do but yank pud.

This job had been a disaster from the top. He couldn't understand; it had all been precisely planned, start to finish, a scam for the scam textbooks. But *every* wheel had fallen off.

Big money, in and out of his hands, just like that. He spit on the pavement. The only consolation, he told himself, was that it couldn't get much worse now.

Reece stood still and watched the orange sun sink into the low clouds. Thinking that maybe this was a sign: time to give it all up, get out of the business, go straight, more or less.

Time, maybe, to get serious about the comedy career. All right, he couldn't really do stand-up—too much exposure for a guy with his past. But why not go to L.A., write some gags for some of those stupid fucking sit-coms? How hard could that be?

Something to think about, anyway. And if it didn't work—well, he knew some guys in L.A. Right now, though, it was Miller time.

Have a cold one and wait, that was the plan. Because people who got on a boat almost always got back off.

Jack throttled the boat down; they stayed in the channel with the engine idling. "So she shot two career drug dealers with long prison records," he said. "Two boys that probably needed killing."

Wesley took off his hat and rubbed his gray stubble. "World's got enough shitbags without those two."

"When I thought you were guilty—" Jack waited for Wesley to meet his gaze. "My plan was to get you out here in the middle of the water, just me and you, and have a moment of truth."

"Meaning?"

"I was going to give you a chance to run, if you wanted it."

Wesley seemed to be thinking it over. "Run where?"

Jack pointed across the water. "See that dock back there? That was your drop-off, with the reporter there waiting for you. You could have told her your story any way you felt like bending, with no witnesses around to contradict you."

"And then what for you? While old Wesley is being chased like the last frog at the frog-leg packing plant? What were you gonna do with the rest of your life?"

Jack took a breath. Then, "I was gonna take your cash to Angelique. She'd go away and never say a word against you."

"I got you." Wesley ran his tongue over his teeth. "You and her, sailing on the S.S. *Sugar Shack*. Tropical ports of call. You, my money, and the wife of mine who was gonna let me go to prison for what she did."

Jack thought it was about to heat up. But Wesley turned away, put his hands on the gunwale, and looked across the water. Saying softly, "Like I told you earlier, probably all my own fault."

"Those two she nailed," Jack said. "As I mentioned, not exactly a loss to humanity."

"That's right. Not like she shot Hank Williams Jr." Wesley cleared his throat. "You gonna make a point one of these days, Jackie?"

"The witness I.D.'d her from the picture you gave me. But so far, the D.A. doesn't have a name."

Wesley straightened, looked, and sounded for a moment like the trial lawyer Jack remembered. Saying, "All they got's a description, then."

Jack smiled a little. "I see no reason for us to do work for the Luster cops."

"Cracker bastards are no friends of mine."

Jack waited. "Still lots of questions, Wesley. I don't think you've been square with me."

"Now, wait a minute—"

"No, it's all right." Jack raised a hand as if to halt him. "Give her the money, let her go, and all the questions stop right here."

The two of them stared at each other. Finally Wesley said, "All right, fine, let her sail away rich. And I suppose you're going with her."

"No," Jack said as he throttled up. "But it's been fun to think about."

The ferry followed the motorboat's path through the channel and then moved into open water. Miranda watched as the boat began to peel to the left. The distance between them was slowly growing.

As the ferry cleared a point off Pelican Island, Miranda saw the sailboat. It had to be the one; the *Happy Family* was headed right for it.

The sailboat was—best guess—five hundred yards away, with the island maybe a quarter mile beyond that. Come on, she swam that far every night just to warm up.

Miranda knew where she had to be. She glanced around quickly to make sure no one was watching. One hairy guy in an Oldsmobile seemed to be eyeballing her for a while, but he finally looked away.

That's when she pulled her shoes off and jumped over the side.

JACK STEERED THE *Happy Family* out of the channel and into open water. He glanced at Angelique's map and turned northwest, Pelican Island to his left. "She sees you're with me," he said, "she's gonna freak."

"Good thinking." Wesley waved a hand at the sleeping compartment below the foredeck. "Old Wesley'll hang out down there, let you handle the opening statement."

Jack brought the boat around a point and said, "There she is." The sloop was in sight. "That look like your boat?"

"That's it. This boy's big mistake, thirty-two feet of floating misery." Wesley opened the hatch and climbed into the compartment. Asking as he went, "Just out of curiosity, Jackie, how you gonna break all this news to Angelique?"

Jack aimed the *Happy Family* toward the sloop. He could feel his heart begin to beat faster. "Still trying to figure that out myself," he said.

The drop was longer than she thought. Long enough for her to see the churning whitewater below her and understand as she fell that she had made a bad mistake.

Miranda went in feet first, with her arms spread. She hit the water like a lifeguard, making a hard downward stroke with both arms, hoping to keep her head from going under. It didn't work.

The inward curl of the wake buried her. She swallowed some water—a strong taste of salt and diesel. The ferry's engines made a thick roar. More bubbles than water here. Miranda tried to swim back to the top, but the force of the water put her in a tumble toward the ferry.

Her head banged against the steel hull. Barnacles ripped at her arms and face. She swallowed more water. Miranda wrapped herself into a fetal position as the ferry moved past her. She didn't know how to find the surface, and she had no air left. The voice in her head said, You're dead.

Then the water jet of the ferry's engine hit her, like a kick in the back. She was propelled, rolling out of control, as if she had been shot from a cannon.

When the water blast finally gave way, Miranda was upright, as if she had been delivered, the light above her. Two strokes and she broke the surface, coughing, then gasping, then coughing some more. She saw the stern of the ferry, moving away.

Miranda was treading water, finding her wind, trying to clear her head, wondering how she'd made it. Her face bled from the barnacles, and the blow to her head had left a throbbing lump.

After a while she looked around. She saw the sailboat and began to swim.

The sailboat caught the evening light, luminous as a pearl. The water glistened. Imagine some coconut palms in the background, Jack thought, you'd have a postcard.

Its sails had been lowered. A small aluminum skiff with a tiny outboard floated about ten feet behind the sloop, tethered by a white rope. From the rear deck of the sloop, Angelique was giving Jack a happy, welcome-aboard wave.

He brought the *Happy Family* to the sailboat's starboard and tossed a twelve-foot rope to a short, dark-haired woman, who tied it to a cleat. She seemed to Jack a little tougher than her snapshot, with small eyes and a thick face that made him think of a snapping turtle.

Angelique, sipping a drink, was wearing a tight white T-shirt above orange bikini bottoms. She smiled and said, "My darling sailor boy." He stared at her—at the smile, at the girlish hair falling over her forehead—and couldn't imagine her in the room at Luster, shooting.

Jack climbed into the sailboat with a callused hand from the dark-haired woman. Angelique said, "Don't hurt him, Lizette." Then she came to Jack and kissed him hard. Her lips were salty from the rim of the glass she held.

"I don't see a package," Lizette said. "I don't see a bag."

Angelique backed away from Jack and mock-frowned. "Neither do I."

Jack looked around the sailboat. Down a couple of steps he could spot the galley. Beyond that were the sleeping quarters. He said, "Angie, there a place you and I could talk for a minute?"

"You know what that means," Lizette said. "Means there's a screw-job coming."

Angelique glanced toward the *Happy Family*, giving Jack a conspiratorial smile. "It's still in the boat. That's what you're about to tell me, right? That you've got it."

Jack followed the look, then came back to Angelique. "Got what?"

She kept her smile, but her voice went steely. "Don't mess with me now, Jack."

Jack put his hand to her arm. She almost pulled away, but not quite. "You talking about the money?" he said. "Yes. It's in the boat."

"All of it?"

"As far as I know."

"Weasel words," Lizette said.

Angelique, staying cool, said, "How much?"

"Count it yourself in just a minute." Jack gestured toward the galley. "First, I have something to tell you."

Angelique uncoiled some and gave him a long, slow blink. "Want a drink?"

"No. Listen . . ." Jack pointed to a deck chair. "At least sit down."

"I think I'll stand."

"All right." Jack felt as sad now as he had ever been, anytime. He was tired of watching stupidity and greed—a pair that loved to travel together—ruin everything. Not that he hadn't consistently done his part to help them. No more. As soon as he was off this boat, Jack told himself, he would find a different way to live.

Now he said, "It turns out there's a witness who saw it all."

A trace of a smile from Angelique. "And?"

"At the motel in Luster, Angie. He saw the shooting."

Lizette shook her head. "All the big buildup for *that*?"

"Bad news for you-know-who." Angelique sipped her drink. She reached for Jack's hand and rubbed the tops of his fingers slowly with her thumb. "All right, you got that off your chest. Now let's do something really fun, like count the money."

Jack felt as if he were a monkey talking to cats. "You don't understand." He pointed to Lizette. "He saw *you* in the room."

"What?" Angelique pulled her hand back and drilled her eyes into Jack.

"That's birdshit from a shitbird," Lizette said.

237

"Angie, he says he saw *you* pull the trigger. On both the victims. I'm sorry."

For an instant no one moved or spoke. Then Angelique stepped closer, her words coming out like steam from a cracked pipe. "Fucking Wesley," she said. "He told you to say this."

"I talked to the witness. I questioned him. He nailed you in a photograph."

Angelique's face twisted in a way he had never seen before. "Oh, boy, he played you like a fiddle," she said. "That's the problem with you soft-headed fucks."

Lizette said, "How much is he paying you?"

"Good question." Angelique moved around Jack to an equipment box.

Lizette said, "You get top dollar for setting us up?"

Jack thought of what he could say now. He could tell them that the Luster D.A. had only a description, with no names and no evidence. That Wesley had agreed not to dime them. That they probably had nothing to worry about as long as they stayed out of one small county.

He could have told Angelique that he might have loved her.

But Jack decided not to say anything. What for? They wouldn't believe him anyway. What he would do now: Get the money, give it to them, and leave. Let them sail away and figure it out for themselves, let himself stagger off and try not to think about it.

Angelique stood and blocked his way. She was holding a .38 revolver, barrel pointed down.

"Where is he?" she said. "That piece of shit I was married to. Where do I find him?"

"Forget it," Jack said.

"He thinks he can do this to me? Where is he?"

Jack wondered what she would do if he kept moving. Then he heard Wesley's voice say, "I'm right behind you, babe."

They all turned to look. Wesley stood on the foredeck of the *Happy Family*. He was pointing a black revolver.

"That piece you're waving around there, Ange, honey?" Wesley gestured with his gun. "Best thing to do right now would be toss it right in the drink."

Angelique said, "I don't think so."

Wesley laughed. "As usual, Jackie, the bitch just won't listen."

Jack went around Angelique to stand between her and Wesley. He said, "Now's when everybody puts their guns away."

"First, this." Wesley swung his weapon toward Lizette and fired. She fell to the deck, screaming, her hands on a wound that was blooming red just above her ankle.

"Next customer?" Wesley said.

Miranda settled into her swim. Good, hard pulls in the water, a solid kick. Even with no wind, the water in the bay was far rougher than her pool. And swimming in clothes was much harder than her nightly skinny-dip; a pair of waterlogged jeans must weigh six or seven pounds.

She glanced ahead every twenty strokes or so to keep herself aimed toward the sailboat. After ten minutes, it didn't look much closer. She must have been fighting a current.

That's fine, Miranda told herself, and picked up the pace. A strong current would make the story better.

Not bad shooting," Wesley said, "for a half-blind old coot."

Lizette lay on the deck, small cries rising from her. A surprising amount of blood was pooling around her knee. In the dim light it seemed to have its own fluorescence.

"Ange, toss that .38 right now"—Wesley motioned with his gun—"or the gal loses leg number two. Go ahead, pitch it overboard, into Davey Jones's locker. Now, that's an expression this old boy ain't heard in a while."

Angelique stood with chest heaving and eyes blazing. Wesley said, "Oh, I feel my finger getting all twitchy."

Finally Angelique threw the gun over the side—a little *plunk* of a splash and it was gone. She went to Lizette and knelt, cradling her head with her arms.

Wesley was still on the foredeck of the *Happy Family*. It had drifted from the sloop, with the twelve-foot rope between the two boats stretched taut. "Pull me in, Jackie."

Jack felt himself falling down another shaft, only this time he saw the bottom waiting for him, and it was cold, hard concrete. He said, "Why did you do that?"

"To get their attention." Wesley waved the gun Jack's way. "Now what I'm gonna have to do to get yours? Pull me in."

Jack didn't move. Bad enough to watch a disaster, worse still, one that you had made. He said, "We need to get her to a hospital."

Wesley shook his head. "You're forcing me into a decision, Jackie. And that would be whether to shoot you or the lovely Angelique. I'm guessing it's ladies first. Unless, of course, you reel old Wesley in, as requested."

Lizette cried some more. Wesley said, "Gonna be a duet of female hurt songs, Jackie, unless you hop." He pointed the gun at Angelique. Asking her, "Which flesh you want your flesh wound in, baby?"

Jack went to the side of the sloop and gripped the rope, then pulled the powerboat closer. "Now back off," Wesley said. Jack moved, and Wesley stepped onto the sailboat. He carried the gun and a gas can from the *Happy Family*.

A weak "Oh, God" came from Lizette.

Angelique gently laid Lizette's head on the deck and stood to face Wesley. "She needs a doctor."

"And old Wesley needs a drink. But both those needs'll have to wait."

"She's losing a lot of blood," Angelique said.

Jack was waiting for Wesley to direct the gun at something besides Angelique. He would go for Wesley then.

Wesley said, "Oh my, I know that look in Jackie's eyes. All those years together in court, I know that about-to-pounce stare. Don't I, Jackie?"

Jack pointed. "Let's put her on the powerboat."

"Oh, yes, I know that look. That's the I'm-about-to-destroy-some-hapless-motherfucker look. Now I know I'm a motherfucker, but do I look hapless? Lucky for me, I got this from that other boat." From his pocket Wesley pulled several pieces of half-inch cord, each about five feet long. "Not much else to do when you're hiding, Jackie, but cut rope and think about what to do with it."

Angelique knelt next to Lizette again. "She's not conscious."

"And here's what I thought of." Wesley threw a section of rope at Jack's feet. "I want you to tie your girlfriend's hands behind her. Turn around, Ange honey, let Jackie work on his bondage skills."

Nobody moved. Wesley said, "Jesus Christ, here we go again." He stepped toward Lizette. "Do I have to finish her off to get some action from you two?"

Angelique stood and turned her back toward Jack. "That's it," Wesley said. "Pick up the rope, my friend."

Jack said, "Stop now, Wesley. While you can."

Wesley put the gun to Lizette's healthy knee. Saying, "Four important words, Jackie, for you to remember: Shut the fuck up."

Jack took the rope.

"There you go," Wesley said. "Now, hands behind you, my darling ex-bride."

Jack wrapped the rope around her wrists, then tied a granny knot that would slip loose with a good tug.

"Hey," Wesley said, "what I look like, the moron du jour? Make it a square knot, the way you learned in the Boy Scouts."

Jack re-tied, not too tight, but snug enough that Wesley wouldn't start shooting people.

"Now her feet," Wesley said. "Lie down, hon. Like you did so many times when Jackie wanted some backdoor."

No response from her. "Well," Wesley said, "it looks like little Lizette needs another."

Angelique went to her knees. Jack tried to help her the rest of the way down, but she shook his hand away. She fell to her side, then rolled to facedown. Jack tied her ankles the same way he had done her hands.

As he finished, she said, "Why did you do this to me?"

Jack wished he knew.

She had come closer now, she was sure, within a quarter mile. A little tired, but nothing she couldn't handle. Her stroke and her kick had stayed strong.

The question wasn't stamina. It was how long Miranda could keep the sailboat in sight. Her biggest problem now was darkness.

All right, you're next," Wesley said. "Turn around, put hands behind your back. Hey, I sound like a cop on TV."

Jack did what he was told. It took Wesley a while, holding the gun. He whistled while he tied.

"That'll do her," Wesley finally said. The rope was tight around Jack's wrists, but not enough to cut off blood flow. He'd had worse.

"Jackie, go get in the captain's chair." Wesley motioned with the gun. "You can sit up there like a grown-up, pretend you're in charge."

Jack went to the chair—a swivel stool with a back—and climbed onto it. Wesley stepped behind him, looped the last section of rope around his ankles, and knotted it to the foot rung.

"You might want to notice," Wesley said, "that this chair's bolted to the deck."

Jack watched as Wesley dragged Lizette and Angelique down the steps and into the galley. "That should keep them," he said as he stepped back onto the deck. He did a theatrical job's-done dusting of his palms.

"Wesley, come on, all these years, they've got to count for something. . . ."

"Oh, they do." Wesley went to the stern and scanned what could be made of the horizon. The sun was a half-sunk orange ball. "Five or ten more minutes'll do the trick," he said. "Then it'll be plenty dark."

He took a battery-operated lantern from a storage box and placed it on the deck between them. It gave off just enough light that Jack could see Wesley's face. He was smiling.

When Wesley wasn't looking, Jack worked at the bindings on his wrists. "This makes no sense," he said. "What you're doing—I don't understand it."

"Couldn't have done it without you, my friend." Wesley winked.

"Done what? And why? You were free, Wesley. The homicide charges were off."

"That's right. All because of that witness. What's his name? Herman?"

Jack froze. Then, "I never told you his name."

"Old Herman," Wesley said. "I'm glad he was so articulate and persuasive with you and the Luster D.A. But, shit, he shoulda been. Cost me five thousand dollars and a fifth of Jim Beam."

Jack was having trouble breathing.

"The look on your face, Jackie." Wesley laughed. "You thought he really witnessed it? You, the master of the cross-examination? Shit, he was passed-out drunk in his shed that night. Three gunshots went off—Herman didn't do a damn thing but snore."

A breeze was stirring, with the whiff of salt off low tide. His mother had always mentioned that on their family beach vacations. She'd take a big breath and say, "That salty air, do you smell it, Jack?" He remembered it now and saw himself as a child, and as the man he had grown into: a guy fated to take the disastrous step no matter which way he walked.

"You know what, Jackie? You're right." Wesley rubbed his scalp, then resettled his cap. "Me and you go way back. Lot of good times together, lots of things in common, including my former wife's midnight love snacks. So you think you deserve an explanation? Well, the clock's ticking. So maybe the short version."

With Jack working at the rope.

Wesley said, "Here's the deal, I was broke. I mean fifty-five years old and stone tapped. How pathetic is that? This boat? The bank'd repo it tonight if they could just find it. Car? They'd take that, too. Office rent was three months in arrears. So one night I'm having a drink with an old client, and he suggests a way out."

The breeze picked up. Jack could see lights on distant boats; none was close. Wesley kept talking: "Client's name was Royal Curley. Agent Reece Pepper to you, which he likes to pretend to be when he's not imagining he's a funnyman. Anyway, Royal had a friend who had a line on two boys with a couple hundred thousand and was looking to buy some heroin."

Wesley laughed and looked away. Saying, "Pretty simple plan we cooked up, really. We set up a meeting with the druggies in a little dogshit town. I show up with a bag of baking soda, supposed to be your contraband. A minute later, Royal, I mean Reece, was to bust in and put us all under arrest. He'd get to flash his badge, which the dumb bastard *loved* to do. Then he'd cuff the two druggies, grab the cash and the phony horse, lead me out the door like I was in custody, and we'd skedaddle. Sure, sooner or later the boys would get out of the cuffs. And what they gonna do at that point? Call the D.E.A. and complain?"

He went to one side and began to haul the dinghy toward the sailboat, hand over hand on the rope. Saying, "A fine plan, except two things happen. Number one, Royal is late, as usual, don't ask me why. The boy's middle name is fuckup. And number two, the druggies had their damn money bag open right on the floor. Probably not theirs, but who cares. More cash in there, Jackie, than you, me, and God's own loan shark ever hoped to touch."

He went down a ladder and into the dinghy. For a minute or so he stayed there, tying the small boat to the *Happy Family*. Jack worked as hard as he could at the bindings on his wrists.

Wesley climbed back into the sailboat with, "Well, I pull my gun and I shoot them both, Jackie. All there is to it. Then I grab the money and head out to catch my ride home. Angelique and Lizette, supposed to be waiting for me in the parking lot. Except as soon as they hear shots, they haul ass, thank you very much. What I'm supposed to do now, call a cab? This old boy has to go back inside the motel room and steal car keys off a dead man." Wesley paused. "He put up no resistance."

Wesley moved to a storage bin at the stern. "All right, make a long story short, I had to hide the money. Which I did. Then I had to dump the car. My trusted assistant Arthur Murry Murray instructs me, leave the car back in Luster so the cops won't be looking anywhere else. Dumbest goddamn thing I ever did, Jackie—I mean *the* dumbest—was drive that car back to Luster. Why was *I* driving it instead of Arthur? To this day, I can't explain it, except to say brain lock. Course, I got stopped for speeding and everything went to shit from there."

From the bin he pulled a five-gallon gasoline can. Saying, "And in the end he screwed me, Jackie. Arthur stabbed old Wesley in the back. Well, you know what had to happen next. Loyalty, Jackie. The most precious thing in life, seems to me."

Jack felt the rope give some. Wesley said, "Brings me to the moral of the story. I've told you this for one reason, Jackie. To show you the extent of Angelique's betrayal."

He pointed to the galley door. "She could have alibied me out of it, she wanted to. But the bitch demanded money to do it. My freedom for a price. That's the message she let you pass along. For two hundred thousand dollars, she and little Lizette was gonna go away, forget she ever knew anything about that motel room."

Wesley unscrewed the tops of both cans. "Wanna hear the funniest thing, Jackie? The kick in the ass? Angelique was on top of the money the whole time and didn't even know it. The whole fucking time, she's sailing around with eight hundred and fifty thousand dollars—did you catch that number, bubba?—right under her nose. I stashed it right here, and she never had a clue." He barked a laugh. "So you see why I asked you to find her."

He picked up one can and turned it upside down, pouring gas on the deck, and then down the steps and into the galley.

Angelique began to scream. Jack pulled as hard as he could at the ropes.

"About time to wrap all this up," Wesley announced.

There was movement behind Wesley. Jack could see something in the water, and then in the powerboat.

Wesley emptied the second gas can into the galley. Angelique kept screaming.

Someone was standing in the *Happy Family*. When Wesley began to turn that way, Jack shouted, "Look at me!"

Wesley cut the turn short and came back to him. "Sure, Jackie, what do you need?"

They locked stares. Jack said, "This is the moment, Wesley, the last possible chance for you to stop."

"I'm gonna light a fire now." Wesley pulled a book of matches from his pocket. "You, I'm sad to say, are scheduled to be part of it. And since you won't be around to care, I'm gonna pin this whole thing on you. All those calls to the marinas, looking for Angelique? I'll make sure the cops know about that, throw in something about a spurned lover. Maybe give them that diary of hers, the parts all about you, anyway."

"Don't do this," Jack said.

"No way to brake this train now."

The smell of gas was all around them. Jack pulled one hand free from the rope, but kept it behind his back. He said, "It doesn't have to end this way."

"Truly sorry it had to come to such a pass." Wesley was three feet from Jack, with the gun in his right hand, pointed down.

Behind Wesley, Jack could see the person in the powerboat, pointing. "Wait, Wesley," Jack said.

Then, from the *Happy Family*, a woman's voice, loud: "You fucking stop right there."

20

SHE HAD FLOPPED INTO the powerboat. Exhausted from her swim, Miranda lay in the darkness. She listened to the men talking, catching what she could. It took a minute or so for her to understand this was not a happy exchange.

Miranda poked her head up enough to see the sailboat. One small light shone there, enough for her to tell that Wesley Joy was holding a gun and pouring gasoline.

This was not the ending that her story needed. A leap from the ferry, and all that swimming, only to watch while somebody got killed? That wouldn't do.

The powerboat had no radio she could use to call for help. And the *Happy Family* was old and fairly small, so ramming the sailboat didn't seem like much of a solution. She wondered if throwing something—thinking, Jesus, what, an anchor?—would do any good.

Then Miranda remembered Kenny Brunson's safety lecture to his foster kids, and the boy who begged to shoot off a flare. She dropped to her knees and began to grope about. Ten seconds, and she found the box she wanted under one of the seats.

The gun felt like a small revolver, but with less heft. Miranda pressed the cigar-shaped flare into the barrel, hoping that she had it right. There was a *click* from the gun that sounded official. She stood, took in the scene quickly, and shouted for Wesley to stop what he was doing.

He did and turned to look. With Miranda thinking, once more, Now what do I do?

She'd had plenty of target practice but had never actually held a gun on a live person before. And unlike the silhouettes she nailed at the range, this guy had his own weapon. A real gun, not a little pop model like the one she was holding.

Miranda didn't even know how tight to keep her finger on the trigger of this thing. Didn't have much of an idea, really, what would happen if she fired it. Wasn't sure what she would do if Joy raised his gun, or if he looked at her and her flare and began to laugh.

All were questions of the sort that Allen the accountant would have asked, while he was doing the Kiwanian No-Balls Dance of the Judicious Man. Screw it. She gripped the flare gun with both hands now, to stop herself from shaking.

"Drop your weapon and put your damn hands way up in the air," she said. Then waited a beat and added, "Fucker."

———

Wesley had snapped his head her way. After a few seconds, he turned back to Jack. Asking, as if they had just met on the street, "This some gal you know?"

At first Jack wasn't sure. Someone stood in the *Happy Family,* that's all he could say. Someone who came climbing suddenly out of the water, like an amphibian in jeans, and flopped into the boat.

The single light from the sailboat had no strength. Jack squinted; he could see that her face and arms were streaked with what he thought was oil or grease. Then he realized: blood.

He said, "Miranda?"

"I'll be goddamned," Wesley said. "It's the reporter girl? That you, darling? Put that silly thing down and let's talk. Better idea, come on over to the boat here and let's fix some cocktails."

Angelique started to scream from the galley again.

"Last time I'm going to tell you," Miranda said. "Put the gun down."

Wesley turned all the way around to face her and asked, "Now, what in the world is that you're pointing?" He began to raise his gun slowly.

That's when Jack jumped. He went up and out from his crouch, could have soared if not for the rope binding his ankles to the chair. It stopped him cold, like a running dog reaching the end of his leash.

He grabbed Wesley as he went down. The two of them fell hard to the deck and lay in the gasoline. The gun was free. Jack grabbed it as Wesley scrambled to his feet.

"Untie my ankles," Jack said. He pointed the gun up at Wesley.

"Goddamnit, Jackie." Wesley was breathing hard through his open mouth. "After all I done for you."

A voice within Jack told him to kill Wesley now. Take him out, and the rest of them could escape. Let him live, the voice said, and no telling what could happen.

But Jack couldn't pull the trigger. Not on Wesley Joy.

"Untie me," Jack said. He flicked a glance toward the rope on his ankles—his mistake. Wesley kicked the gun from his hands. It skidded across the deck. Wesley had it in a second and stood over Jack with the barrel pointed down.

"After all I done for you," Wesley said again. "And all you done for me." The gun was pointed at Jack's face. Wesley said, "This'll wrap it up just right, Jackie."

There was a *whoosh* and streak of sparks, as if a small comet had zoomed into the boat. The flare hit Wesley in the ribs and drove him into the open galley door. Wesley and the sparking flare fell down the steps.

The galley was instantly on fire.

Jack twisted onto his back, sat up, and untied his ankles. He stood just as the gas on the deck ignited. Jack tried to dance away from the fire and get to the galley door. All he could see inside were flames.

Then came an explosion, the galley's propane tanks. The whole deck was on fire. Jack's clothes were starting to catch. He had nowhere to go but over the side.

Miranda stood in the *Happy Family*, staring at the fire. Saying aloud, "Oh, Christ, what did I do?"

She tried to find a fire extinguisher but couldn't. When she saw Jack jump into the water, she attempted to start the engine—no go. So she untied the boat and paddled to him. The light chop of the bay reflected the orange of the flames, as if the water itself were on fire.

With her help, he climbed into the boat. "I'm sorry," she said, the only words she had. The sailboat was all flames now, heat rolling over them as if it were a giant open furnace.

"We gotta get to shore," Jack said. He looked at the dinghy, tethered to the *Happy Family*. "We'll use the five-horse."

He pulled the dinghy in close, jumped in, and went to work on its small outboard. Then he was back in the *Happy Family*, clamping the dinghy's motor to its stern.

While he worked, the fire roared. Miranda couldn't tear her eyes from it. She remembered the photos of earthquakes and the disasters she had yearned to see. She had never thought it would be like this.

Jack pulled the starter cord on the small engine. After ten or so tries it finally stuttered to life. He guided the boat, achingly slow, toward Pelican Island.

"We'll cut past the point," he said, "and head across the channel to the Coast Guard station."

Miranda said, "Hurry."

There was an explosion from the sailboat. "Fuel tank," Jack said.

They skirted a jetty, then stopped moving with the sound of metal grinding against rock. Jack glanced toward the dinghy. "Came too close," he said. "Got the rowboat stuck. We'll leave it here."

He cut the engine and freed the dinghy's rope from a cleat. Then they were moving again, the small boat left behind.

"Look at this," Jack said. He was bent over a nylon bag, muttering, "Here it is, the great treasure that killed everyone."

Jack knelt, opened the bag, and pulled out some newspapers.

"Come on, get up. What are you doing?" Miranda yanked at his wet shirt. "We need to hurry. We need to get help."

"Help what?" Jack stood and looked back at the flames. "There's nothing left."

21

BY SIX THE NEXT evening, Reece Pepper was working on his fifth beer and third pickled egg at the Sportin' Life. He had been there long enough that the bartender wouldn't pretend to laugh at his jokes any longer. Fine, like he could give a shit. All Reece was doing now was waiting for the sun to go down.

He thought about the stash. According to the late, great snitch Arthur Murry Murray, Wesley had said it topped eight hundred grand. Might be that much, might not, might even be more. What it wasn't, Reece knew, was burned up.

Sure, he'd heard people talking right there in the bar about the boat that flamed to the waterline last night. Newspaper said three people died.

There also were two survivors. Which meant the cash was still part of this life. Because nobody let that much money go up in smoke. Somebody had to have it.

Best bet was Flippo or the reporter. Reece figured he would try the chick's house first, once she was sure to be in bed. Maybe he would get lucky and find them both there. Oh, man, let the fun begin: pistol-whip party time, until somebody talked.

He finished his beer and listened to his last selection from the jukebox—"Tulsa Time," by Mel McDaniel—then gathered his change from the bar and slid off the stool.

The evening air hung thick and warm as Reece walked out the door of the Sportin' Life. He crossed the parking lot toward his Explorer, whistling and thinking that there were worse ways to spend a few hours than torturing a couple of assholes. Telling himself that if he couldn't pound the money out of them, nobody could.

Only question was whether he should pack a bag for his immediate departure once he had the money in hand. Or should he just peel a few bills off the swag and buy everything new? That would be fun.

Life, the thought, could start to look good in a hurry. Just like the old joke: Man sees his mother-in-law standing beside a wishing well. She falls in. Man says, Who knew those things worked?

Reece was laughing to himself as he reached his Explorer. He was opening the door when he heard a voice say, "Yo, Curley."

Two guys stood ten feet away. Both of them were pointing guns at him. And one of them was flashing a federal badge.

Reece went for his own gun, which brought his comedy career to a sudden halt.

They had spent most of the night and all of the following day at the police station, answering questions. Now they sat by the pool in the dark, drinking a lot but not talking much. Finally Miranda said, "God, I killed three people."

"No, you didn't," Jack said. "You saved the life of one person. That would be me."

"I just meant to scare him with that flare. Throw him off somehow, make him drop the gun. Not kill them all." She began to cry.

Jack rose and went to her, put his arm around her shaking shoulders. "Time to get some sleep," he said.

He led her inside. The back door stayed slightly ajar, but who cared? No one worried about air-conditioning bills at a time like this.

In her bedroom, Miranda turned off the lights and curled up on the bed. "I need someone to hold on to me," she said. "You're the only one around."

He lay next to her, under the covers, his arms around her. Within a few minutes her breathing told him she was asleep.

No such luck for Jack. He stared into the dark and faced the understanding that *he* was the one who had killed them.

His blundering steps had brought them to that moment on the boat. His failure to act had sealed it. When he had a chance to cut the losses by shooting Wesley, Jack lost his nerve.

Now he looked at the clock—after midnight. He stared into the dark some more. When he finally fell into sleep, he had nightmares of Angelique's screams and the smell of burning flesh.

He was suddenly awake, with the screams gone but the smell still there. Something sharp was pressing against his chin. A man's voice said, "Where the fuck is it?"

Miranda heard talking and opened her eyes. Thinking, something strange, not sure what, better turn on the light. She reached to the nightstand and switched on the lamp. A scream came out of her before she could stop it.

A man, his skin scorched and blistered, stood over Jack. His clothes were partly burned away. The one eye patch was gone, nothing but a blackened socket left. He smelled like death.

He said, "Ask you one more time, Jackie. Where the fuck is it?"

"You're hurt bad," Jack said. "You need a doctor, Wesley."

"Only one thing I need, and you know what it is."

Miranda kept her eyes on the man as she slowly moved her hand beneath her pillow.

Jack had seen burned people before, but never one this bad who was still walking. Wesley looked like someone who should have been buried two days ago. Asking Jack, "How much of your throat I'm gonna have to cut?"

He felt Miranda's fingers against his, beneath the blanket, and then the gun in his hand. Jack gripped the handle. He didn't even know if the gun was loaded.

"They got hatches on the front of them boats, Jackie. Flames were licking my ass, but I got to the hatch in time. That propane blew just as I was climbing out."

Jack said, "Too many of us have died, Wesley."

"Don't think so, not really. Couple more might need to go." Wesley's hand was trembling. Jack could feel the knife cut a little deeper into his chin.

"You need help, Wesley."

Wesley said, "Only thing I need, Jackie, is get what's mine."

The knife went deeper still. Jack raised the gun beneath the bedspread. This time he pulled the trigger.

The Galveston cops kept him for six hours. Jack told them the same thing over and over: "He had a knife at my throat. He was about to kill me."

The session ended with Lieutenant Torres saying, "You're starting to make me sick, you know it?" And, "When you walk out of here, my friend, the first thing you do is get your ass gone off this island. For good, forever."

Before he left, Jack was informed that the shooting of Wesley Joy would be referred, as a matter of routine, to the grand jury. No sweat there, he thought—self-defense all the way. Witness Miranda Glass would be his walking ticket.

Now, just before dawn, Jack was in his police-auction Chevy, flying over the deserted road across Pelican Island. Telling himself, Only one reason Wesley would have come back.

He was less than a mile from the submarine park when he pulled his car to the side of the road. He got out and, with his flashlight, thrashed his way through the brush to water's edge. Thorny branches tore at his face and clothes. The night sky was beginning to seep away.

Jack used his flashlight to sweep the shoreline, a gentle slope of sand covered by boulders of broken concrete: dead buildings and bridges, torn apart and dumped here to keep the place from disappearing one boat wake at a time.

His light went up and down the phony rocks, but he found nothing. Jack walked a few yards toward the point and swept with the light again. That's when he saw the aluminum dinghy—wedged between two chunks of concrete, right where he'd left it.

He started to run to it but tripped after four or five steps, his foot catching on a crooked piece of rusted rebar. The fall ripped a nasty gash in his skin, but Jack got up and ran again.

An unseen piece of driftwood staggered him but didn't take him down. Another ten yards and more rebar caught his ankle. Jack kept going. By the time he reached the boat, he was sucking in air as if he had sprinted a mile.

The dinghy was a third of the way onto land. Jack shined his light from front to back; the boat was empty. One last chance, he thought. He stepped into the boat; it rocked a little and scraped loudly against the concrete.

Jack leaned against the center seat and pulled the lid off the bait well. Inside were two black plastic garbage bags.

He tore at the plastic until he had seen all he needed to see.

At dawn, Kenny Brunson was behind the bait shop, swabbing the deck of the *Happy Family*. He scowled at Jack's approach. "One thing I teach my boys," Brunson said, "when you borrow something, you put it back better than you found it."

Jack set a suitcase on the dock and squatted next to it. "Good lesson to learn."

"Ropes were all cut up and the gas tank was gone," Brunson said.

Jack popped the latches on the suitcase. "How much?"

"What? I don't know." Brunson hauled himself onto the dock and wiped his hands on his pants. "I replaced the gas tank with a spare. The rope—well, rope is cheap. Cost of the damage is not the point, know what I'm saying?"

"Yes, I do. What I'm asking"—Jack opened the suitcase lid—"is how much for the whole boat?"

Brunson stared as Jack opened one of the black plastic garbage bags inside the suitcase. Both of them gazed into stacks of bills.

"Take this." Jack slid the suitcase toward him." It's supposed to be somewhere around eight hundred grand. For your boat. Keep the change."

Brunson cut his eyes from the money to Jack and back. Jack jumped into the boat and said, "Take it, and don't tell a soul."

He started the Evinrude. It coughed blue smoke and died. He tried it again and the motor caught.

Jack untied the boat and looked across the flat calm of the bayou. Silver and pink water mirrored the sky. "I'm sailing off into the sunset now," he said.

Brunson, on his knees next to the suitcase, scanned the horizon. "Believe that's the sunrise."

Jack nodded and turned the boat that way. Saying as he went, "It'll have to do."

SEP 1 0 2001

WYTHE-GRAYSON REGIONAL LIBRARY
1000147852

M SWA
Swanson, Doug J.
House of corrections
1000147852

WHITETOP PUBLIC LIBRARY
WHITETOP, VA. 24292